M000014502

About the Author

Jeong Sik Choi majored in Film Production at university and pursued a career in advertisements as a music director, copywriter, and creative director. In 1989, he received an award in a writing contest hosted by the Korean national Broadcasting Station which inspired him to pursue writing. He published his book 'New York Blues' in 2002. The novel gained attention for being the first book to be published with its own CD soundtrack, just like many movies which have their own. Jeong Sik is currently working as a stock-trader and resides in Auckland, New Zealand and Seoul, South Korea.

Jazz Lovers

Jeong Sik Choi

Jazz Lovers

Olympia Publishers
London

www.olympiapublishers.com
OLYMPIA PAPERBACK EDITION

Copyright © Jeong Sik Choi 2021

The right of Jeong Sik Choi to be identified as author of
this work has been asserted in accordance with sections 77 and 78
of the Copyright, Designs and Patents Act 1988.

All Rights Reserved

No reproduction, copy or transmission of this publication
may be made without written permission.
No paragraph of this publication may be reproduced,
copied or transmitted save with the written permission of the
publisher, or in accordance with the provisions
of the Copyright Act 1956 (as amended).

Any person who commits any unauthorised act in relation to
this publication may be liable to criminal
prosecution and civil claims for damage.

A CIP catalogue record for this title is
available from the British Library.

ISBN: 978-1-78830-868-7

This is a work of fiction.
Names, characters, places and incidents originate from the writer's
imagination. Any resemblance to actual persons, living or dead, is
purely coincidental.

First Published in 2021

Olympia Publishers
Tallis House
2 Tallis Street
London
EC4Y 0AB.

Printed in Great Britain

Acknowledgements

This novel started with a small storyline that I thought of while I was watching a Pat Metheny Group's concert. The group's pianist, Lyle Mays, and guitarist, Pat Metheny, have had a lot of influence in my life. While I wrote this novel, I always had their music by my side, and I want to say thank you to those two people.

English isn't my first language so, in order to finish the final product, I needed a second pair of eyes to proofread this work in detail. Thank you, Mrs Barbara Baragwanath, Samantha Pyo, and Aaron Choi for kindly offering to help me. And thank you to the editorial team of Olympia who made the final touches to this work.

1
Early Autumn 2014

Hyun Suk watched the doctor through a chink in the curtain around his bed. The doctor was peering intently at his computer screen. Hyun Suk sensed bad news. It occurred to him that this was an important moment in his life. This was it.

The doctor sighed, arose from his chair, and came towards him. Hyun Suk lay back and pretended to be asleep. He was barely ready for what was coming. Soon, he felt better. Everything was going to be all right.

The doctor came over to his bed and saw him sleeping. He returned to his computer.

Not wanting to deceive him anymore, Hyun Suk opened his eyes and cleared his throat. The doctor looked up...

"Ah, you're awake now."

Their eyes met.

"I fell asleep," said Hyun Suk, raising himself on his pillow.

The doctor sat down beside him and looked at him quietly for a moment. Hyun Suk knew what was coming. He tried a cheerful expression, briefly to encourage the doctor to speak.

"I'm really sorry, sir. You have come to this clinic too late. You need to be transferred to a major hospital right now."

Hyun Suk took himself outside. He lit a cigarette. It was the first time he'd smoked in four months. Steady rain was falling. Perhaps it wanted to help him put out his cigarette.

He found some shelter and lit up again. Now, he really had broken his promise to himself. He pondered how he had overcome that addiction. But nothing could overcome his broken life.

He didn't return home, but went in another direction, not caring where he was going. He wandered aimlessly in the hustle and bustle of the city. After a while, he noticed passers-by were looking at him. What did they see? A man over sixty with long hair in a ponytail? How did they see him? Ragged, deathly white and unstable? Walking with a limp, without an umbrella, he went down into a subway to escape the rain.

"*Munsan Station*, please." He had to ride three different trains.

Three is quite the task for me right now, he thought.

Hyun Suk climbed into a crowded train. He couldn't reach any of the handles and lost his balance. People brushed against him. He grabbed onto a strap near the open door. A girl near him covered her nose with a look of distaste. He must have smelt dirty. He lost his grip, unbalanced and disoriented. The girl was glaring at him, so he backed into a corner behind the glass door panel. The train shook. Hyun Suk leaned his forehead against the glass. A fierce wind blew his baggy clothing and he kept losing his balance. He looked like a scarecrow in a huge swaying field. The train entered a dark tunnel. The scarecrow entered his dark night.

2

Hyun Suk came down from the loft with two objects in his hands. It was a Haegeum (a traditional Korean instrument similar to the violin) and bow (similar to the bow of a violin). He placed the instrument on the floor and went back up into the loft. He had forgotten something. He came down with two spools of string loosely wound on each reel – one for the Haegeum and the other for the bow. He then put them down beside the instrument. He sat there, looking intently at them. He kept looking at them for a long time. His eyes shifted across to the belt of lead weights on the floor, his face was an image of deep sadness.

Eventually, he sat up, his jaw set in determination. Picking up each lead, he tested its weight on the belt and checked each of the other items lying there. His gaze settled on his clothes and he suddenly registered an oversight—he only had one change of clothing. He went over to his wardrobe and took out more clothes. Hyun Suk then gathered the things from the floor into two separate bags. Everything was ready, but there was one more thing that he had forgotten. Going to his desk, he opened the drawer and took out a letter. He read it again, calmly checking the words to see if anything was missing. He stood up and stared blankly at the picture on the wall. It was the only one in the room and it was a picture of his family— his granddaughter, son, and daughter-in-law. His eyes misted over then he became calm again.

He heard his son, Jeong Soo, calling.

"Bye Dad. See you tonight. We're going out now."

Hastily, Hyun Suk put the letter into his chest pocket, picked up the two bags, and pushed them into his wardrobe.

"Have a nice day!" he called back, opening the door.

There in the courtyard, his daughter-in-law, granddaughter, and Jeong Soo were on their way out.

"Oh, just so you know, I'm off to *Choon Chun* for a few days," Hyun Suk said.

Jeong Soo and his wife stopped and looked at one another, taken aback.

"Are you? Why *Choon Chun*?" Jeong Soo sked.

"Oh, I've got some things to get done there."

3

Choon Chun, South Korea

Hyun Suk followed the porter into the hotel room. The porter put the bags down. Hyun Suk said to him, "I need your help with something."

He took some money from his wallet and handed it to the porter.

"What's this for?"

"I'm going to *So Yang Lake* for a few days. Could you please post this letter for me, to my home address?"

The porter hesitated but took the letter. Thanking him for the money, he left the room.

Hyun Suk looked around him. Through the window of the room, he could see the lake and mountain. It was early autumn. The leaves slowly blended into a beautiful shade of red and yellow.

The next day, he woke up early and opened the curtains. The weather had changed, and the sky was now overcast, a strong wind blowing. He stood gazing at the lake for a long time.

Three bottles of soju were on the table. One was already empty. Hyun Suk poured himself another glass from the second bottle and downed it.

Placing the two bags over his shoulders, he picked up the Haegeum and left the room.

Hyun Suk was up on the mountainside, not far from a cliff. From there, he looked down at the great, rocky expanse below where he could see the lake; its waves rippling in the wind. He saw a big tree on the slope, a short distance away. He headed towards it. When he got there, he placed his bags on the ground at the foot of the tree.

He went on towards the cliff edge and sat down. There was a fierce wind blowing all around him, but he barely noticed it. He went back to the tree and took a bottle of soju from one of the bags. He gulped it down, then took out his Haegeum and bow and placed them on the ground. He lifted the spools from his bag and started to unravel each spool in order to attach the strings onto the Haegeum and bow. It took a while to tie the strings onto the instrument. He then wound the rest of the loose string back onto the spool. As he tried to put them back in the bag, they didn't quite fit. They fell out, rolling a little way down the hill. Hastily, Hyun Suk ran down after them. Because they were round, they were being blown in all directions by the wind and it took him a while to catch them. He didn't even notice that the strings of the spools were becoming tangled around his leg. When he managed to retrieve both spools, he carried them back to the tree and laid them in one of his bags. Sitting down, Hyun Suk took another gulp of soju, wiping his mouth on his sleeve. He then took the Haegeum and bow and prepared to play. His hands were shaking, but he managed to tune the instrument. He began to play. Even though it was a traditional Korean instrument, the tune he played was entirely western in spirit. At first, the sound he made was a little rough, but soon it settled into the most exquisite and moving melody...

When Hyun Suk finished playing, he laid the Haegeum on the ground. With a look of deep sadness and weariness, he stood up. He swayed giddily, affected by the alcohol. He removed his shirt and looked down at the lake again. He then picked up his Haegeum and bow and tried to put them back into his bag. They didn't fit into the bag, so he took the spools and weight belt out and rearranged them. As he was doing so, the excess string of the Haegeum knotted around the weight belt and the spool, tightening around his ankle as he approached the cliff edge. He was still unaware that his leg was tangled in the Haegeum string or that his bow strings were caught up in his weight belt. With every step he took, the strings became taut. Next, Hyun Suk checked the strength of the weight belt that he had made. Anyone watching him would have started to understand what this desperate man was about to do. After he put his weight-belt down on the ground, he drank some more soju. As Hyun Suk lifted the weight belt and put it around his waist, the loose part of the bow string that hung out of the bag got caught between the joints of the lead weights on the belt. He moved closer to the cliff edge. At that moment, Hyun Suk caught sight of his birth town on the horizon in the distance. He gazed in its direction and slowly knelt in a gesture of deep respect, bowing his head to the ground. After a short while, he quietly stood up and approached the cliff edge. His eyes focused on the waves in the lake below him. His legs suddenly began to tremble violently. He closed his eyes. His legs of his trousers flapped in the wind, prompting him to leap.

Hyun Suk sighed, took a deep breath, and jumped...

But as he fell, the strings that were knotted around his leg and waist, together with the Haegeum, the bow, and the bag, all followed him down.

All of these items became lodged in the protruding branches of a tree which, as luck would have it, was growing in the middle of the cliff face. The weight of these objects stopped his fall, halting his body with a powerful jolt. It knocked him twice against the cliff face. His neck and hip bore the brunt of the impact.

Hyun Suk screamed. With one foot caught in the branches, he dangled head down in mid-air after crashing against the cliff face, way above the waters of the lake. Blood streamed down his shoulder to his face. There were cuts all over his body. His hand reached for his shoulder and when he pulled his hand back towards him, he saw that it was covered in blood and loose skin from his wounded shoulder. As he hung there, he tried to find the place at his waist where he felt pain but couldn't reach it. His hand flailed desperately around in the air.

4

Hyun Suk's body, drenched in blood, was being quickly wheeled by emergency staff on a hospital trolley towards the operating theatre. A woman walking past happened to glance down at him. Startled, she put her hand to her mouth in shock as she caught sight of the massive blue birth mark covering his buttocks. Suddenly, she froze. Turning to look at him again, she peered, transfixed, as he was being wheeled away. She remained gazing after him down that corridor for a long time. The woman's name was Yeon Mee Choo.

Yeon Mee walked towards the waiting room outside the emergency theatre. She sat down in a daze, staring at the floor. Several times, she rose and went to the desk to ask for the name of the patient. At first, they would tell her nothing, only saying that they did not know. She returned to the desk again and again with the same request and finally, they gave her the man's name. Over and over in her mind she had been asking herself whether that man could really be Hyun Suk. From one moment to the next, she wavered between wanting it to be Hyun Suk, and wishing and hoping that it was not him.

5

1982, Thirty-two years before, *Choon Chun, South Korea*

There was a wooden house. It appeared to be quite run down and barely lived in, but from inside came the sound of someone playing lively modern music on the piano.

Inside that house, there were ten Yamaha pianos with a student placed in front of each one. Among them, only one student was playing; she was a girl. Her name was Yeon Mee. She happened to be playing a piece by Kenny Dorham called *Blue Bossa* (Joe Henderson's *Page One* Album, 1963). The piano teacher, who was also her father, and the rest of the students gathered around Yeon Mee, watching as she played. One of them, an older fine-looking student, was internally applauding her playing. That student's name was Hyun Suk. Even after Yeon Mee finished playing, the clapping continued for a long time. She rose from her seat modestly and bowed to them. Her eyes met the eyes of Hyun Suk. She was shy – her cheeks blushed like a peach, a soft pink.

Yeon Mee was twenty years old. She was elegant and slim. Her neck was slender, and her eyes were brown, bright and beautiful. The teacher rose from his seat beside Yeon Mee and began to speak.

"Even though this is my daughter, I have to say that her fine playing of *Blue Bossa* certainly demonstrates the excellence of jazz!" The students smiled at this, and some of them laughed. Their teacher, Mr Choo, spoke again,

"Now it's time to explain ragtime—a genre of musical composition for the piano. I know I mentioned it briefly last week. Has anyone practised it yet?"

Only one of the students raised a hand.

"It's you again, Jee Hoon. Didn't anyone else practise it?"

When nobody replied, Mr Choo continued,

"Well done, Jee Hoon, even after such a short explanation of Ragtime last week. Tell me, which one did you practise?"

"Scott Joplin," he replied shyly.

"Good, let's hear it now."

Jee Hoon thought for a while then carefully placed his hands on the piano. He focused on the melody, with his right hand, while his left accompanied with syncopated chords in the style of ragtime.

Hyun Suk's house was in front of a circular courtyard where his father had his Haegeum workshop alongside the house. In the centre of the courtyard were all the tools of his trade. On the right was a room where the Haegeums were painted, and on the left was the area where Hyun Suk's father cut the wood to make the instruments. His technique was perfect—he was a master craftsman. In the front of the courtyard, Hyun Suk's mother and older brother, Hyun Meen, attached the completed Haegeums onto a wire frame to dry.

The Haegeum teacher, Hyo Jun, appeared at the entrance to the courtyard. He looked for Hyun Suk's father, who was a little surprised to see him. Hyun Suk's father asked, "What brings you here? Come in please."

Hyo Jun looked ill at ease. He was lingering by the

entrance to the courtyard, so Hyun Suk's father walked over to him. Hyo Jun glanced uneasily towards Hyun Suk's mother and brother, reading their minds. He opened his mouth quietly.

"I have come to talk about Hyun Suk."

"Is anything the matter?" Hyun Suk's father enquired.

"He didn't come to class last week."

"He didn't? He missed class again?"

"Yes," replied the Haegeum teacher, a touch of scorn in his voice.

"He has applied to go to that piano academy once again."

Mr Choo opened his bag, took out a vinyl record, and announced, "Today we'll listen to the album I promised you last week. The song we'll listen from it now is *Wave* (Antonio Carlos Jobim, 1967). I told you about it before. So, do any of you remember who pioneered bossa nova?"

"Antonio Carlos Jobim," chorused the students.

"Right, well done. Bossa nova is the greatest genre of music in the history of jazz. Jazz can hardly be expressed in words, but if I really had to explain it, I would say that jazz expresses beauty and happiness. Did you know bossa nova actually means not only sadness, nostalgia, and romance, but also infinite beauty and happiness? Antonio Carlos Jobim is by far the best exponent we have of bossa nova. His music expresses the meaning of life, which as we all know can be sad and beautiful, or even happy. So now, let's listen to his song."

The teacher placed the vinyl on the record player. First, they heard the prelude, then the main melody. Mr Choo noticed that the students were talking to one other and looking at Hyun Suk as the music progressed. The atmosphere was lively, and they were listening, happy and attentive, which brought a smile to their teacher's face. He was pleased to see how involved they were in the music.

When the music ended, the teacher asked them for their impressions of what they had just heard. They all said that they loved it. Then one student spoke up and said,

"Actually, we have heard this before."

"Really? When was that?"

"Before you arrived last week, Hyun Suk was playing it."

"Was he really?"

Mr Choo looked over at Hyun Suk, raising his eyebrows questioningly.

About one year prior, the teacher remembered that Hyun Suk had played the *My song* (Keith Jarrett, 1978) entirely without the score, playing by ear. The teacher realised at that moment that Hyun Suk was indeed a highly talented musician, and since then, he had followed his progress with great interest. However, he also knew that Hyun Suk was set to become the next generation's major exponent of traditional Haegeum music. He had already acquired the technical expertise to become a master craftsman of Haegeum instruments, which was his family's heritage. Therefore, he knew that Hyun Suk's father would expect his son to follow the tradition of the family business and therefore, Hyun Suk would not be able to continue with the piano. Despite all this, Hyun Suk had returned to the piano, so his teacher was all too aware that his interest in the piano was in direct conflict with the wishes of his family.

Suddenly, the teacher very much wanted to hear Hyun Suk play *Wave*. He assumed this student would be able to play that piece by ear as well.

"So, Mr Hyun Suk, do you played *Wave* often?"

21

He shook his head.

Mr Choo repeated his question,

"Have you ever seen the *Wave* score?"

He shook his head again.

"Then did you play it by ear after hearing it on the radio?"

Hyun Suk nodded.

The teacher pointed towards the piano with his chin. Hyun Suk hesitated a moment then walked over and sat down in front of the instrument. Just as he was about to play, he heard a cicada singing outside the window. He got up, went over to the window to close it, and returned to the piano. He took a deep breath, sighed, and then began to play. He played with perfect ease and grace. From the very first note, it was as if he had been playing it all his life. His playing was close to the perfection of the original recording even though he was only an amateur pianist. He picked up on the song's distinctive soft rhythm that sounded like a smooth pebble being thrown across the surface of a lake, gently touching here and there. All the students looked at one another, surprised at the skill he displayed. Yeon Mee smiled at him. Her father could hardly bring himself to smile as he absorbed the meaning of this brilliance in amazement. He frowned, thinking to himself, 'How can he do this so well? I just can't believe it.'

At that very moment, just as he had those thoughts, there came the harsh, angry sound of someone kicking open the door, shattering the hinge as he did so. It was Hyun Suk's father, Yong Ju. Enraged, he carried a wooden stick in his hand.

He approached his son at the piano, brandishing the stick and yelled at him, "Damn you, have you forgotten that you should be practicing the Haegeum for the competition? Why are you here? You shouldn't be here. You shouldn't be playing that bloody instrument at all. You should be at home where you belong, practising a superior instrument. Get up at once! Leave right now!"

Hyun Suk froze. He looked down, deeply embarrassed and humiliated. He didn't move from the piano. His father started ranting again, shouting at the top of his voice. He waved the stick again and stared in fury at his son.

"Get up. Get out. Immediately!"

His son still did not move. The father then whacked the stick down hard on his son's shoulder. The teacher rushed to intervene, grabbing the father's arm. Yong Ju pushed him aside roughly, slamming him against the wall where he fell to the floor. Yeon Mee rushed to her father's side. Hyun Suk stood up. His father's rage was subsiding. But his parting words were harsh, intended more to insult the teacher than his son.

"You know hundreds of musical scales, so why waste time on a pathetic few that is, no more than the number of your own fingers and toes?"

Hyun Suk defiantly gathered up his music to put it in his bag but his father, with a renewed surge of anger, grabbed the music violently and ripped it to shreds. Hyun Suk watched him with a look of hatred and despair. His father then took him by the collar and dragged him over to the door. Yeon Mee followed them helplessly, a look of deep compassion for Hyun Suk across her stricken face.

6
The present

The hospital.

Hyun Suk lay on the bed, sleeping. Yeon Mee sat, watching him for a long time. Someone knocked on the door. Yeon Mee called,

"Come in."

A nurse appeared, carrying some things.

"The police gave me this. It's his personal belongings."

There was a box and two bags. Yeon Mee went over to look at them. Inside the box was the broken Haegeum. In the bags she could see clothes with blood on them. She felt afraid. Something fell from a bag. It was his wallet with money tumbling out of it. As she stuffed the notes back in, her eyes caught sight of a photo. It was of herself, thirty years ago. She picked it up and looked at it closely, an expression of deep sadness and longing came over her face. A profound melancholy filled her. She thought about how, long ago, she and Hyun Suk had been lovers. They had kept their love a secret from others. Their love for each other had been deeper and more sacred than anything else in the whole universe through millions of years. She remembered how beautiful their love was, and here she was, after all these years, seeing him again. What a tragic day it might have been, but instead, this unexpected happiness had come back into her life. Was this her destiny? To have him back in her life. Yeon Mee looked at the photo of herself again. Suddenly, she was jolted from her reverie by the sound of her mobile phone ringing. She went out of the room with her phone. At that moment, as she left the room, Hyun Suk's eyelids fluttered slightly.

"Hello?" Yeon Mee said.

"Where are you?" it was Sung Jae.

"I'm sorry love, I couldn't call you because I'm at the hospital."

"The hospital?"

"Yes, something has happened. Someone I know has been admitted to hospital urgently."

For a second, he did not talk.

Yeon Mee said, "I'm really sorry. Has your mother arrived already?"

"Yes, she has."

She detected a flash of anger in Sung Jae's voice.

"Sweetheart, I'm so sorry, it's entirely my fault. I'm really sorry."

"Are you telling me you can't come here now? I don't know who is in hospital and I don't care. If he is not your father then you should be here. I hope you understand." And then Sung Jae hung up. Yeon Mee held onto her phone for a while, staring at it, then hung up. She was thinking that she should really go to be with Sung Jae's mother. He was furious with her, but she also wanted to go back to be at Hyun Suk's bedside so very much...

A nurse was inserting a needle into Hyun Suk's arm. He opened his eyes and looked around him, wondering where he was. He watched the nurse disappear out into the corridor.

Someone was in his room. He looked at her.

"Excuse me, but who are you?"

Yeon Mee smiled at him.

"Who are you?" he asked again.

"It's me."

"Who?"

"It's me, Yeon Mee."

Hyun Suk, dazed, tried to raise himself on his pillows, staring at her.

"Don't you know who I am? I am Choo Yeon Mee."

"Choo… Yeon Mee?" he said incredulously, and for a long time they looked at each other in silence.

Yeon Mee kept her smile. Hyun Suk stared at her in disbelief.

All his life he had been dreaming of her, his great love, greater even than his love for his only son and his granddaughter. Their love mattered less to him than his lifelong love for Yeon Mee. And here she was. He could not believe it. Only this very morning he had tried to take his own life… he had not expected to meet her again on this earth. For the last 30 years, he had drawn her face in detail in his imagination and had looked deeply into her delicate features as he drank. He had thought he could love her a thousand-fold forever more. But this beautiful woman was not a dream. She was there at his bedside, right now, and she was looking lovingly at him. He was speechless. He just gazed at her, his lips trembling.

"We met thirty years ago," said Yeon Mee gently.

"Thirty-two years ago," said Hyun Suk.

Yeon Mee smiled.

"Why are you here?" asked Hyun Suk.

"Are you feeling better now? I saw you being wheeled into Emergency."

"I have spent my life longing to hear from you," whispered Hyun Suk.

"I can't believe that I found you here," Yeon Mee spoke softly to him.

"I heard that you had gone to Japan. So why are you here in *Choon Chun*?" Hyun Suk asked.

"I've been here for two years." She was going to explain her situation further, but at this moment, she didn't feel like her long answer would be appropriate. Instead, she gently asked Hyun Suk a question.

"Why did you do what you did this morning?"

Hyun Suk didn't reply.

"You don't need to answer," said Yeon Mee, trying to be light-hearted.

They were silent for a while. Then Hyun Suk asked her, "What brought you here to this hospital?"

"My father is having medical treatment here. I met with his doctor this morning and on the way out I happened to see you."

"How did you know it was me?"

When she did not reply, he asked again,

"How did you know what I looked like after thirty-two years?"

Yeon Mee said with a little smile,

"You were naked. I saw your backside!"

He understood what she meant. He asked,

"Has your father come back from Japan?"

"Yes, my father wanted to be buried in his home town."

"He wanted that?"

"Yes, he did... and then... is he okay?" Yeon Mee changed the subject abruptly. Hyun Suk nodded. He knew she was asking about his son.

"What's his name?"

"Jeong Soo," he replied.

"That's a lovely name. Do you have only Jeong Soo?"

"Yes. I never married. I remained single. I'm just an old bachelor."

Yeon Mee's eyes registered surprise. He looked down and silence fell between them again.

Hyun Suk raised his head, a questioning expression on his face. Yeon Mee looked into his eyes and understood.

"Yes," she said, "I have been married, once. My husband died long ago. I have one daughter. She left home early to marry. What about Jeong Soo? Is he married?"

"Yes, I have one granddaughter."

"She must be lovely. Um... Does Jeong Soo know anything about me? Talking about him made me curious."

Hyun Suk hesitantly opened his mouth.

"He doesn't know. Your name and even your age."

A look of deep regret passed over Yeon Mee's face. She asked,

"What does Jeong Soo do?"

Hyun Suk was quiet for a while, then said, "He plays the Haegeum, like me."

They were silent again. Hyun Suk became dejected suddenly as soon as the Haegeum was brought up in the conversation. Yeon Mee saw the look of depression coming over him, and, trying to be positive, asked,

"Are you still wearing the ring?"

Reluctantly, Hyun Suk said, "My finger is fatter now—it

isn't easy to take it off."

Yeon Mee smiled a little, then said seriously, indicating the photo from his wallet,

"Has this photo always been in your wallet?"

Hyun Suk looked at her shyly, then said,

"I was thinking about my home town, coming here, so I took that picture from my photo album…"

"It's in such good condition even though it's over thirty years old. You must have taken very good care of it, all these years."

Hyun Suk said nothing but blushed and looked down.

7
The Past

It was evening. Hyun Suk got off his bicycle, leaned it against the wall, and headed for the gate to his house. He heard a voice coming from the woods somewhere.

"Hi Hyun Suk!"

"Yeon Mee?"

"Yes, it's me. It's been ages."

"Yes, it has. It's been quite a while, Yeon Mee."

Hyun Suk was happy to see her again, but he didn't dare come too close to her yet in fear that his father might see them. He looked around anxiously, then went nearer.

"Why have you come up here now? It's very late."

Yeon Mee handed him one of the things she had been holding.

"I came to give you this. I got it for you. It's *Balanco no Samba*!"

"Oh really?" His face lit up, "Is it from the *Big Band Bossa Nova* (Stan Getz 1962) on Stan Getz (Jazz saxophonist) album?"

"Yes, I also got *Intermodulation* (Bill Evans & Jim Hall, 1966) and *Undercurrent* (Bill Evans & Jim Hall, 1962). I remember that you always had an eye out for the song, *I've Got You Under My Skin* (Cole Porter 1936), and I found it on the *Intermodulation* album."

Hyun Suk's eyes opened wide in surprise.

"How did you find these?"

"I got them through one of my relatives who lives in Japan. And the song *Samba De Verao* (also known as *Summer Samba*, 1964) from Marcos Valle, which is really hard to find in Korea, will arrive next week."

Hyun Suk was very happy. She took her bag from her shoulder and pulled out something. She passed it to Hyun Suk, saying, "I've been learning the score at the Piano School for the past month."

Hyun Suk looked at her in wonder and opened the score. There, he saw it was written by hand in her small and tidy writing. He looked into her eyes, speechless with thanks. She saw that he was very moved.

"I was thinking, as I was transcribing this score," she said, "that maybe you don't need it. Maybe you would not have the chance to play a piano, but anyway, I wanted to write it for you."

He gazed at her. She was looking in her bag again for something else.

"And this is some coffee for you, I know it's your favourite. There wasn't a bigger one, so I got the small one."

He didn't move at all.

"Don't you want it? It's for you," she tried to make him take it.

Hyun Suk was embarrassed and unwilling to receive more gifts.

"Have you heard about our concert coming up?" she asked.

"Here are four tickets. I thought you might be able to come even though I know your father disapproves. I wish you could come. I'll be there."

Hyun Suk remained silent, overwhelmed. But Yeon Mee took his hand in hers, pressed the tickets into his palm, and said, "I have to go now."

She didn't want to let go of his hand.

"I really must get going," she said at last, turning away from him. She walked slowly back in the direction of her home.

Hyun Suk felt the same way. He didn't want to let her go, and so he tried to speak,

"You came here to give me all these things? Is that the only reason you came?"

Yeon Mee looked back shyly at him.

"No, that's not the only reason. I haven't seen you for so long, I wanted to see you."

After a long silence she hesitated, then said,

"But I really should go." She moved away again.

Hyun Suk was thinking how especially lovely she looked this evening. He felt he had lived a painful life as if dipping his foot into ice-cold water. Since Yeon Mee had come into his life, it was as though a fresh and comforting spirit had settled all around him. Today she had appeared, bearing so many gifts: three albums, a score, coffee and then tickets, all for which he felt so grateful. However, there was one thing she had said that was more priceless than any gift, and that was, 'I haven't seen you for so long, I came here to see you.' He had never heard such a declaration since he first met her. He wanted so much to give her something too, something very secret and very special. Quickly he called after her.

"Yeon Mee, wait. Can't you go back home later tonight?"

She interrupted him quickly, "Sure! Why not?!"

Hyun Suk and Yeon Mee climbed the hill together by torchlight. It was rocky and steep. She slipped and stumbled, then stumbled again, hoping he would catch her, help her, and he did. He caught her arm, and she leaned against him, staying there longer than she needed to. Hyun Suk gently moved her away. He was afraid to go too far with her too quickly, so he tried to control himself, but she clung to him.

"Careful, don't trip. Don't fall in the lake. Listen, can you hear the ghost of *Soyang Lake?*" he said. Yeon Mee was nervous and stayed close to him. Once again, he tried gently to distance himself a little.

At the top of the hill, they could see across to an old house.

They went inside. Power cords were dangling all over the place like a spider's web and a light was on. Yeon Mee wondered at this, and then in surprise, caught the sight of a piano. It was a very old one. How had it managed to get all the way up here? She looked around the room, gazing at the pictures of jazz musicians and the shelves full of albums and books.

"Are you surprised?" he asked.

"How have you done all this?" she exclaimed. "Where did you get the piano?"

Hyun Suk didn't reply but went over and picked up a *Stan Getz* album.

"This is my secret place. You mustn't tell anybody about it."

Yeon Mee's eyes fell on a picture of a Harley Davidson on the wall,

"That's a nice bike!" she said.

"Do you know Harley Davidson?"

"My cousin rode one when we were living in Japan."

"Really? Have you ever heard the sound of a Harley engine?"

"Yes, I know what you mean. Maybe you like the sound of the engine more than the bike itself?"

She was very perceptive, he thought to himself, surprised that she read him so well. Most people assumed when he mentioned a Harley that he just wanted the bike, not the sound it made. He said,

"Ever since I was a child I've always thought about the sound of the piano and the sound of Harley engines. And I've always loved those two sounds."

"Do you have another sound you love?" she asked.

Hyun Suk looked at her, curiously,

"Haegeum!" she cried.

He gave an embarrassed smile.

"Yes, that's right. The Haegeum sound is nice, but you know, it doesn't have to play only traditional Korean music. Western music sounds great on it too, really magical."

"Have you ever tried that?" she asked in delight.

"Yes, I have. Many times."

"Really? That's amazing! Western music on the Haegeum!" she looked across at the Haegeum leaning against the wall, "Play it for me, please. I'd love to hear it."

Hyun Suk wondered what her favourite instrumental piece was in her own repertoire. He asked if there was any favourite piece that she would like to listen to.

"Oh, Michel Legrand's *I Will Wait for You* (A song from the French musical *The Umbrellas of Cherbourg,* 1964)," she replied.

"Go on, you play the piano, and I'll play the melody on

34

the Haegeum."

She looked questioningly at him, wondering how the two instruments would sound together. Yeon Mee began to play first, then indicated to Hyun Suk to begin. Straight away, she understood how perfectly the melody matched the emotion in the piece. Suddenly, she stopped playing and looked at Hyun Suk.

Hyun Suk asked, "Why did you stop?"

"I am so taken with the quality of the sound of the Haegeum. It's fantastic."

Happily, Hyun Suk suggested changing the rhythm to bossa nova. Yeon Mee couldn't imagine how the Haegeum could be played so quickly, in harmony with the piano, but soon she knew she was mistaken. As soon as she began the bossa nova rhythm, Hyun Suk joined in effortlessly with the melody.

They had a wonderful time together that night, making music, feeling so happy and contented. They finished playing and smiled at each other. Hyun Suk was sweating. He went towards the stereo player and put on the record of Stan Getz' *Big Band Bossa Nova* album. As the song *Balanco No Samba* started playing, Hyun Suk spontaneously got up and began to dance the samba with all his heart and soul. He found that he wasn't at all shy of dancing in front of her.

8

The piano teacher, Mr Choo, was sitting at his desk opposite the window when somebody knocked on his door.

"Come in!"

The door opened and Hyun Suk appeared.

He bowed his head respectfully and greeted the teacher.

Mr Choo was definitely not happy to see Hyun Suk. He remembered, all too well, the outrageous behaviour of the young man's father. It had been the most absurd thing he had ever seen in his life.

"Why are you here?"

"I have something I want to discuss with you."

"Sit down," said the teacher abruptly, indicating the chair in front of him.

Hyun Suk put his Haegeum bag down and sat.

"What would you like to discuss?"

"I heard about the jazz festival."

"Yes, it's next week."

"I would like to join the festival."

"Ah, Hyun Suk, if I let you do that, your father would come at me with a big stick and kill me! I'm really sorry, but it can't be done. In any case, enrolments are full. Hyun Suk, I'm sorry, but you must leave," urged the teacher.

"But I wouldn't be playing the piano. I'd be playing the Haegeum."

Amazed, the teacher said,

"But this isn't a traditional, classical Korean festival. It's a jazz festival!"

"I know that, I understand completely. It's jazz that I'm going to play on the Haegeum!"

9

The Present

All his life, Hyun Suk had never stopped dreaming about Yeon Mee. Every waking moment, he had been obsessed with her. She was his muse. He had filled the emptiness in his soul by imagining that she was always by his side. Hyun Suk had two hearts. One that belonged to Yeon Mee, and the other one was also dedicated to her. She had been deeply rooted in his heart deeper than the Cretaceous strata. Thirty long years had passed, during which he never stopped thinking of her as the centre of his life. From time to time, when feelings of despair and worthlessness trapped him in despondence, he would clasp onto memories of loving her to try to lift his spirits. He never wanted to let go. And yet in the past and even in the present, she slipped into boundaries beyond his reality. In this case of love, the realities of life always offered up intangible barriers. He knew that. He had tried to accept this harsh reality. He kept thinking to himself, 'How much did I love her then?' and 'How much do I love her now?' He tried to bear it all courageously; getting up, shaving, eating breakfast, and going on and reading the paper.

Now, Yeon Mee was coming into his room, carrying a fruit basket in one hand and a suitcase in the other. She was earlier than expected. Hyun Suk looked at the clock, wondering why she was so early.

"Good morning! How are you?" she asked.

Hyun Suk was sitting up in bed.

"Nice to see you!" he said.

She put down the bag, smiling at him,

"You look much better this morning."

He smiled at her, "Yes, much better." He touched his neck and waist.

It had been three weeks since they had seen each other. But there was still silence and awkwardness between them.

He asked her, "Do you think I could change rooms? I'm not comfortable being in here."

Yeon Mee was unwrapping the fruit basket.

"Please stay where you are." Yeon Mee insisted.

"No, this room is too luxurious for me."

"Why don't you change into these clothes?" she asked, taking some garments out of the suitcase.

"I thought you'd be too busy looking after your father," Hyun Suk said gratefully, "why did you come so willingly to help me?"

Yeon Mee, placing the fruit in the fridge, smiled awkwardly.

"Please don't feel obligated towards me," she said, "this can't last much longer."

There was a silence...

Looking out the window, Yeon Mee observed, "The weather's good today."

"Yes, it's a nice day," he said, also looking out the window.

"Would you like to go out?" she asked.

Hyun Suk smiled and nodded.

"Why don't we listen to some music?" she said as she drove him along in her car.

He smiled. She knew that his smile always meant 'Yes'.

"Here's a British fusion jazz funk group. I've got their song ready for you. It's a beautiful song with a lovely beat that is slightly melancholic. The group is Shakatak (English jazz-funk band)! Have you heard of them?"

She could see by the look on his face that Hyun Suk had indeed heard of the group.

"So, you know them?" she asked, happily.

"Absolutely! They're a legendary cross-over jazz band. I really love the way Bill Sharpe plays the piano. He makes a great sound with just a simple melody."

"What's your favourite song from this group?" she asked him.

"*Invitations* (*Invitations* Album, 1982)."

"Wow! Do you have another?"

"*Night Birds (Night Birds* Album, 1982)."

"Oh my God! That's exactly the one I've chosen. It is my absolute favourite song. I love Bill Sharpe just like you. Could you please tell me about any other jazz pianists that you like?"

"Lyle Mays (Jazz keyboardist, best known for his work with guitarist Pat Metheny and his group). Do you know him?" he asked.

"You're kidding. He is also one of my favourites!"

"Like Pat Metheny, Lyle is also a genius... And another jazz pianist I love so much is Hirotaka Izumi (Japanese jazz keyboardist)."

"T Square's (Japanese fusion jazz group) Hirotaka?"

Hyun Suk was surprised. He went on,

"Yes right. Exactly! All the members of T-Square are

perfect, but he made them even more beautiful. And just like Hirotaka, Lyle made Pat Metheny Group's music sound extraordinary too. The way he plays the piano; it's like he's from another planet."

"Amazing! It doesn't feel like we have been separated for 32 years. It feels like we've been living together! Lyle's piano in *Au Lait* (Pat Metheny Group, *Offramp* Album, 1982) is the best music of my life… And I believe Hirotaka's ability to play the piano has made my life richer than ever before."

"I am so glad. I can't believe you like them just as much as I do. Do you have any more?" he asked.

"Do you know Gilson Peranzzetta (Brazilian composer and jazz pianist)?"

"Of course, I do!"

"Have you heard the music from the *Brazilian Scandals* album (Oscar Castro Neves, 1987) he participated in?"

"I've heard of it. That's another legendary album," he answered.

"I love all the songs in the album, but *Pensando* is the best. Gilson's piano in the song is simply amazing."

They looked at each other in awe. They could not believe their unanimity.

"Do you still enjoy Keith Jarrett?" she asked.

"Why wouldn't I? Have you heard of the 2009 Berlin version of *My Song*? I really love it. It has the best intro ever. Sometimes I even play his *Tokyo Solo Part2d* on the piano."

"I know both! *Part2d* is really beautiful. He seems to have surpassed human limits."

There was a silence between the two and they did not want to break it for a long time.

Finally, she said, "Why don't we listen to Shakatak's

song? Should we go for *Night Birds*?"

Hyun Suk said, smiling, "Let's hear it when we reach the top of the hill."

Yeon Mee pulled the car over and parked when they were at the top. There was a lovely view over a large lake. Her hand reached for the play button...

Today, for the first time since they met up again, Hyun Suk had a smile on his face. It was as if he had been woken from a nightmare. Yeon Mee was glad she took Hyun Suk out for some fresh air despite the protests of a senior nurse. It was clear from his face that he had wanted the outing so much. His smile today was his gift to her.

There were two coffees placed on the coffee table.

"I haven't drunk coffee for so long, I'd forgotten how good it was." Hyun Suk said, and he went on, "Actually, it was because of you."

Yeon Mee looked at him in wonder.

"Ever since that day, long ago, when you came with gifts and gave me coffee, I haven't been able to drink it any more. I thought of you every time I had it. For me, it was all too much – what it symbolized. You do remember, don't you? That you brought me coffee?" Hyun Suk said.

Yeon Mee searched her memory. She said to herself, "Yes, it's true, I did do that." She looked into his face and saw that his gaze was so fixed on her, as if he was a sculpture, with such intensity that she turned away to look out the window. There was a long silence

Finally, she said,

"Can I ask you a question?"

He turned his face towards her.

"Why did you do that?"

He wondered what she meant. Again, she asked,

"What you did that day? Why did you want to leave this world?"

Hyun Suk looked down. Then, he looked away towards the horizon and didn't speak for a long time.

"How can I give you the right answer?" he said.

She waited.

"I just felt that I had so many problems. Life just wasn't worth living any more, I thought I would be better off dead. Should I answer your question like that?"

Then, Hyun Suk remained quiet for some time, sighed deeply and said,

"I wanted to experience the crossover between life and death."

"Crossover?"

"My life had always seemed like a living death. Death has always been a very real part of life for me."

He went on.

"If I hadn't met you at the hospital, I still would be at that boundary between life and death."

Yeon Mee tried to understand what he was saying, tried to imagine what it would be like to experience such a close link between life and death, which was plainly the reality for Hyun Suk.

10
The Past

Town Councillor's Office.

Yong Ju's mouth dropped open in shock and anger at the town councillor's words.

"There is more. As you know the place that we wanted for a Haegeum School is now going to be a Piano School. We also know that the mayor supports the Piano School."

"Councillor," protested Yong Ju, "the mayor promised us a Haegeum School at the last election. There were many who witnessed his speech when he made this promise. He has broken his promise. I won't sit here and let that happen! I've put a lot of effort into that Haegeum School over the past ten years."

The town councillor said,

"Please come to my place and bring the Haegeum teacher, and we'll talk through this problem."

Yong Ju frowned. The town councillor went on,

"Would you like to go to the music festival tomorrow? Even if you don't want to, it might be wise to because the mayor is going to be there. Let's re-assess the situation tomorrow."

The next day.

On a stage in the grounds of the school, there was a student playing the piano surrounded by other students playing various instruments, such as an acoustic and electric guitar, drums and bass. Above the stage was a banner, *'Celebrating Our Jazz Festival'*. An audience of about three hundred was assembled on the lawn in front of the stage. Some sat on the grass, some on newspapers or portable chairs. There was enthusiastic applause after each performance. Yong Ju's family was seated in the middle of the audience. The clapping went on for a long time, but Yong Ju's face was clouded with distaste, especially as his wife and his eldest son were both applauding. He was not pleased with them, and they stopped clapping when they sensed his annoyance.

The commentator introduced Yeon Mee next. She appeared on the stage. Many people clapped as she sat down at the piano. As she played, people were calling 'Bravo! Bravo!' Yong Ju looked at them all as if they were out of their minds. "Crazy people," he muttered. Yong Ju felt miserable. He couldn't understand this sort of music and it irritated him. So, he looked up at the sky, trying not to listen, and puffed on his pipe. Yeon Mee played a reverse turn beautifully, with a lively beat. Two young women near Yong Ju spontaneously stood up and began dancing. They were dressed in fashionable western clothing with low necklines, and Yong Ju didn't like the look of them at all. Suddenly, he lost his temper and got up and struck the two young women on the head with his pipe.

"You're being disrespectful in front of your elders! And you're wobbling your hips as if you're old ladies! Didn't your mothers teach you how to behave? Get away from here!"

The girls looked at each other in bewilderment. Then one of them touched her head where she had been hit, put her other hand on her hip, and taunted him, saying,

"Hey, old man, you can't say that to us!"

Yong Ju was shocked at this outrageous lack of respect. It dawned on him that his masculinity was being insulted but also that these young women weren't just common girls as he had thought at first. He turned to his wife and eldest son saying,

"I can't stand this anymore. Let's get out of here! This isn't a music festival; it's just a perversion of music. And where is Hyun Suk anyway? Go and find him."

He was speaking loudly and his family, embarrassed, ignored him and remained where they were sitting.

"Get up!" He demanded loudly again. The whole audience was now looking at the interruption caused by this family. Yeon Mee was very much aware of what was going on as she played. She could hear Yong Ju losing his temper. The mayor got up from his seat in front of the stage, annoyed and angry at the disruption, and glared across at Yong Ju. The town councillor, seated next to him, waved his hand at Yong Ju to silence him and make him sit down, not wishing him to provoke the mayor. Yong Ju did as he was asked and sat down. He looked at the ground, humiliated.

Yeon Mee finished playing. The audience applauded. She stood and bowed to them. The commentator then appeared on the stage to introduce the next player—Yang Hyun Suk. Yong Ju had been looking away at the mountains. He turned towards the stage and stared, dumbstruck. His son was walking across the stage. His wife and elder son stared at each other in amazement. They had no idea that Hyun Suk could play Western music. They both found that their legs were quaking with nerves and their hearts were thumping. Hyun Suk was carrying his Haegeum. He sat on a chair, ready to play, watching Yeon Mee at the piano. Part of the audience clapped. Others were whispering to one another, "this is a jazz festival!" Yong Ju couldn't move his body as if his limbs had become paralyzed and his face became white with shock. He gazed motionlessly at the stage, refusing to believe that the man who appeared on the stage with a Haegeum was his own son.

Yeon Mee's melody began on the piano, and Hyun Suk played the Haegeum alongside her. They were playing a song called *How Insensitive* by Antonio Carlos Jobim. Yong Ju glanced at the mayor to see what he was thinking about Western music being played on the Haegeum. Another person in the audience was astonished. It was Hyun Suk's Haegeum teacher. He and Yong Ju looked at each other…

Hyun Suk was halfway through the song. Most of the audience had never experienced Western music being played on the Haegeum before. They remained tense, unfamiliar with the sounds they were hearing. Some, however, responded emotionally with 'Bravo!', their eyes shining with surprise and delight. One man in the audience was concentrating intently on Hyun Suk's playing with a look on his face as if he was witnessing The Creation itself. That man was Mr Choo, the teacher at the Piano School, and Yeon Mee's father.

It was only a week before that Hyun Suk had gone to Mr Choo's office. He had asked if he could play jazz on the Haegeum at the upcoming festival. At first, Mr Choo had not been at all sure that bossa nova jazz could be played on the Haegeum, but Hyun Suk had demonstrated that it could. Mr Choo called on other instruments to accompany Hyun Suk to provide the melody and rhythm. However, Hyun Suk had insisted that only Yeon Mee should play with him and finally Mr Choo had agreed, understanding how much it meant to the young man. Also, he understood that Hyun Suk's playing was extraordinarily powerful. He, in turn, insisted that there were to be only two rehearsals before the festival. But above all expectations, here they were together, playing unbelievably well and completely in harmony with each other. Hyun Suk's playing was exquisite, and some in the audience were shouting with excitement. But just as they were beginning the final refrain, a voice from the audience shouted.

"Stop that music!"

Hyun Suk's heart sank. He recognised his father's voice.

"Stop!"

Yong Ju burst onto the stage. Yeon Mee and Hyun Suk froze, aghast. Yong Ju went towards his son, grabbed him by the collar and dragged him off to the side. At the same time, the town councillor and Mr Choo also ran up. The town councillor caught hold of the Yong Ju's arm to push him away. Behind him, Mr Choo was exclaiming angrily,

"What do you think you're doing? Right in the middle of their performance? This isn't gentlemanly behaviour!"

Yong Ju hissed at Mr Choo, "You say I'm not behaving like a gentleman? What about you? You're enticing my son away from his true vocation. He is a traditional musician, and you make him play this garbage music! What's gentlemanly about that? And why are so many people here? They should be out working in the fields right now. It's harvest season. What kind of shitty festival, shitty behaviour is this?"

Yong Ju raised his voice even louder, turning to the crowd, "Our time is precious, we have to work. You people out there!" he cried.

Yong Ju rolled up his sleeves, preparing to fight Mr Choo.

"I'm warning you. You should know that this town is

dedicated to traditional music! Why are you contaminating it with this western nonsense?"

Hyun Suk's Haegeum teacher followed Yong Ju up on to the stage and shouted,

"He's right, ladies and gentlemen, where else is there a town like this one? For generations, our town has followed traditional values. We should be playing only traditional music here, not Western music."

The town councillor then spoke up to the Haegeum teacher, saying,

"Just a minute, Mr Haegeum Teacher, why do you have to support Yong Ju at this moment? Don't you realise who is at this festival? Don't you understand that your behaviour is disgraceful?"

Yong Ju and the Haegeum teacher stared at each other, surprised to see that the town councillor taking the mayor's side.

The town councillor tried to force Yong Ju and the Haegeum teacher off the stage, but Yong Ju was stronger and stood his ground. Yong Ju then tried to push his son off the stage once again. The mayor rose from his seat. The mayor and Yong Ju eyed each other, both very angry.

Two years before, the mayor had promised Yong Ju a Haegeum school in the town. That was why Yong Ju had been a long-time supporter. He was devoted to him until the election. But Mr Choo, although later than Yong Ju, had also supported him even financially during the elections. Eventually, the mayor and Mr Choo became friends. Since then, the mayor gradually changed his mind about his promise and rumours began to spread that he was now in support of the idea of a Piano School instead. Yong Ju had confronted him angrily at the time, and the mayor no longer wanted to meet with him at all. This was the greater reason behind Yong Ju's violent indignation today, beyond the fact that he had found his son disobeying his wishes.

The mayor picked up his jacket and left the concert, accompanied by the town councillor and another official. Other people in the audience also got up and left. Mr Choo then lost his cool completely. He saw Yong Ju pick up a chair and throw it towards the piano. Mr Choo ripped off his jacket, rolled up his sleeves, and the two began to fight in earnest. All the musicians, along with Yeon Mee and Hyun Suk ran towards the men, trying to stop the fight but couldn't. Others from the audience ran up on to the stage to help.

Finally, the two were separated. Mr Choo had a swollen lip, and blood coming from his mouth. Hyun Suk's father had a bloody nose. Hyun Suk, with the help of others, held his father in his grip. Yeon Mee, with the help of others, held on to her father. Both men were breathing heavily, eyeing one another. Yong Ju spat at Mr Choo and it landed in his left eye. All of them froze in shock.

#

On the table were many large bottles of soju.

Yong Ju was sitting across from the Haegeum teacher, who was saying,

"Well, Yong Ju, how can we make Hyun Suk understand? I don't know what to do any more. Last year, he was spending so much time playing the piano that he dropped a grade in his Haegeum examination." Saying this, he felt a surge of anger again and said even louder,

"I don't understand. Why is he doing that? How can he like jazz more than Korean music? I just can't understand it! If his grades continue to drop, he will lose his last chance to become a cultural asset to this nation."

There was an angry silence. The Haegeum teacher went on,

"If Hyun Suk passes this examination, we would have so much more influence with the mayor to get the Haegeum School for this town. And of course, your son would gain great honour."

Yong Ju slammed his glass down on the table and said,

"I hit my son several times yesterday because he told me that if I didn't let him play the piano, he'd stop playing the Haegeum as well. He's crazy, completely crazy! If he keeps going like this, I'll cut off his fingers!"

#

Hyun Suk's secret place.

Hyun Suk was sitting in the long mountain grass, pondering. The river flowed below him. Behind him was his secret house. On his face were bruises and blood from his encounter with his father. He stood up and went inside.

He sat down at the piano. For a few weeks now, he had been thinking about what gift he could give to Yeon Mee. He began to understand that the best possible gift for her would be a sheet of music. He began to compose. With great happiness, he thought how this deed was the finest thing he could do for her. After she had come so lovingly to him, it was time he did something for her too. After his father's terrible attitude and behaviour, Hyun Suk knew that, perhaps, it was unlikely that he would be able to continue spending time with Yeon Mee. He assumed this musical score would be the first and last gift from him to her. Anything less than this would be meaningless.

In his mind, Hyun Suk had been building a boat composed of a jazz melody. Very soon, he might have to sail far away from here. The gift he was preparing for Yeon Mee brought comfort to his troubled mind. It helped him cope.

#

The Korean Traditional Instrument Place of Practice.

About thirty students were sitting around, practicing together as an ensemble. Hyun Suk was amongst them. His face was still scratched and there was bruising around his eye. They finished playing the score. The Haegeum teacher stood up and said, "I don't think anybody has been practising much lately, am I right?"

He continued, "I do understand that you all have to help with the harvest, but you know we really need to practise more than ever at the moment. Are you all being a bit lazy? If we go on like this, we won't be able to win any prize, and we'll never get the Haegeum School. What will people think of us then?" his voice registered great disappointment. He looked over at Hyun Suk and saw he was looking out the window instead of paying attention.

"Hey, Hyun Suk!" he called, annoyed. He repeated, "Did you hear what I said?" Hyun Suk looked at him, saying nothing. The teacher spoke to everyone,

"We don't have much time, you know, we have to practise more."

Hyun Suk was looking out the window again. More annoyed than ever, the teacher called him again,

"Hey, Hyun Suk! Still looking out that window, not listening. You've made two mistakes already in one song because you're not paying attention. I suppose you've got jazz on your mind, have you?"

Hyun Suk still said nothing.

"Do you really mean to perform the exam in front of the master judge playing like that? You should think of your family and your father."

Hyun Suk looked with defiance at his teacher. There was a chilling atmosphere in the room now. The Haegeum teacher turned his attention on the other students. He said,

"Let's start that piece again now."

Hyun Suk placed his Haegeum into its bag and headed for the door. The Haegeum teacher swore quietly at him. Hyun Suk heard him and looked back at him with disgust.

"Why have you got that look on your face? Am I wrong in what I said?" said the teacher.

Hyun Suk was suddenly overcome with sadness.

For several years, Hyun Suk had been moving between playing the Haegeum and piano. That was exactly why the Haegeum teacher had been persecuting him. He understood his teacher's position, so he was usually able to feel some sympathy for him, to feel less resentment against him. However, this time he had had enough.

"I'm sorry, sir, but there are many kinds of music in the world, and all are still music. Please stop rejecting other kinds of music. Please stop thinking I'm crazy just because I love playing jazz and piano too. Why do you do it? I have another question for you. Why are you so crazy about Queen and their bass guitarist, John Deacon? What is the difference between you and me? We both love music, don't we? Why the hostility?"

The Haegeum teacher fell silent.

Hyun Suk opened the door and walked out.

#

At the home of Hyun Suk's family, Hyun Suk's father stood outside in the courtyard. His mother was there too and Hyun Suk himself was beside the house, at the rear. They were all working on oil painting the Haegeum instruments.

Hyun Suk's brother appeared at the main gate, and just behind him was a young lady. She was looking away, shyly, with her head down before his parents.

His mother went over to Hyun Meen and the young woman.

"Hello dear, please come in."

She turned to her son, saying,

"Why don't you two just come inside?" Hyun Meen took his girlfriend's hand and brought her into the courtyard. He took her over to Yong Ju. Eyes cast down, she bowed before the father, saying,

"I'm pleased to meet you. My name is Ju Hee Seo."

Hyun Suk's father stayed seated and looked the girl up and down. He looked displeased. He was grumpy and didn't reply to her greeting.

After a while, he said,

"Yes, I've heard about you already. You would like to marry my son? So, why are you dressed like that?" at this, Hyun Suk, his mother and brother all became very uncomfortable and tense.

The young woman was wearing a modern yellow suit and matching yellow heels. They knew what was coming. Their father didn't like the western dress. He preferred the traditional Korean style. He was looking her over again with displeasure. He stood up and disappeared out the back of the courtyard. Their mother quietly took her elder son by the hand and whispered to him,

"If only you could have told her to wear a traditional Korean dress today!"

"I didn't because her mother had bought her the suit she's wearing especially for today," he replied.

Hyun Suk continued painting a Haegeum, overhearing the conversation. He got up, pursed his lips, let out an exasperated sound, and threw his paint brush on the floor.

Yong Ju returned. He was carrying a heavy load which he put down in front of Ju Hee. There were two large plastic containers. One contained a knife and two chopping boards. The other had Korean cabbages, white radishes, a cucumber, garlic, chilli powder, young radishes, spring onion, ginger, salted shrimps, salt, and pine nuts. All the ingredients needed for kimchi.

"There," he declared. "Now make five varieties of kimchi. If you need more ingredients, I will supply them."

Yong Ju's family looked shocked and embarrassed. Hyun Meen looked at his mother in disappointment. She returned his look silently, shaking her head.

Hyun Meen said to his father,

"Father, this is the first time Ju Hee has met you. It's not fair. She is unprepared to have to make kimchi. It's too much for her."

But Ju Hee said in a strong voice, "I will try. I will do it right now."

She removed her jacket and placed it over the back of a chair. She took off her high heels, her stocking, and asked Hyun Meen's mother for some waterproof shoes. She then dragged the large plastic containers over to the shade and began to work.

Hyun Suk watched her throughout. He felt deep sympathy for his brother and his girlfriend. He tried to imagine what it would be like to introduce Yeon Mee to their father.

It took five hours for the kimchi to be prepared. At last, Ju Hee put the dishes on to the kitchen table. There was square radish kimchi, cabbage kimchi, watery kimchi, pickled scallion kimchi, cucumber kimchi, pickled young radish kimchi, and another dish. The father just said, brusquely, "Why did you make seven when I told you to make five? What's this one?" he continued, "I've never seen it before."

Ju Hee replied, "I made salted vegetables with the leftovers."

The father tasted every dish critically, one by one…

He looked across at his wife. Everyone in the family was there, looking tense. He merely asked,

"Do you have leftover steamed rice? All the kinds of kimchi are very delicious."

They all breathed a sigh of relief. Ju Hee had passed the unexpected test.

11
The Present

Sung Jae began to smoke more frequently. Some people smoked to relieve stress or depression. Others smoked recreationally, just because it made them happy, regardless of the fact that it may be a habit or addiction. Nowadays, Sung Jae's reliance on smoking seemed to come from his suffering. He was feeling distressed and hurt, not sure any more of what Yeon Mee really felt towards him. She had mentioned a few days before that Hyun Suk was her lover long ago. Did she still love him or was it a crush and just simply memories from the past? Sung Jae felt perplexed. Yeon Mee seemed to be avoiding coming to meet his family. They had already made preparations for their wedding. Now, there seemed to be a cloud of swirling doubt around all this. Now that this fellow Hyun Suk had come on the scene, things seemed to have changed. He felt Yeon Mee had definitely become distant towards him. He felt upset. Why? Was something secret happening between her and this man? Was she hiding something from him? However, all of this was only in Sung Jae's imagination.

Today, Yeon Mee had told him she wouldn't visit Hyun Suk any more. Today was to be the last time that she would see him. Sung Jae felt a huge surge of relief upon hearing this news. Perhaps, all would be well between them now. Surely, he could be a better lover to her. Thankfully, his feelings of inferiority, jealousy, and suspicion were receding. He began to feel much better, the taste of his cigarette today turned out to be a happy one. It was the best cigarette he ever puffed!

And yet, the happy moment was not to last. Anxiety came creeping back and he began to lose confidence again, in spite of all the positive signs.

Sung Jae exhaled out the car window, "Is he really better now?" he asked.

"Yes," she replied quietly. She looked out the car window into the night. Sung Jae wanted to know her feelings. He wanted reassurance.

"How am I looking?" he asked her, "Have I lost weight?"

She looked at him, saying nothing.

"I was feeling heart-broken, and I was forgetting to eat," he said. Yeon Mee gave him a little smile with her eyes.

"I'm really sorry about what's been happening lately—your family and everything, especially your mother," she said sadly.

"It's all in the past now," he assured her. "Don't worry about it. Just come and meet my family. Last time, when you didn't come, my mother said, 'Even if she has changed her mind totally, please understand. Perhaps she might be in a difficult situation, beyond her control. Try not to be too hard on her'."

Yeon Mee felt very moved hearing about the kindness of Sung Jae's mother. She looked out the window again, then back into Sung Jae's eyes, her lips trembling. He saw that she was now looking brighter, and he turned the key in the ignition.

Sung Jae parked his car right outside the hospital where Hyun Suk was staying. He looked at Yeon Mee. She didn't get out of the car. She just sat there.

"Well, we're here," he said.

"Thank you for driving me here, Sung Jae. I was meaning to come alone," she said.

Sung Jae remained silent, then said,

"Even though you really wanted to come alone, I would have brought you here," he said firmly.

She sensed passionate feelings rising in Sung Jae. She got out of the car and went over towards the front door of the hospital.

She entered Hyun Suk's room. He didn't notice her at first. He was looking at his Haegeum, thinking about the repairs he would have to undertake. She came towards him quietly, then sat down near the door and watched him silently for a long time. Then she spoke,

"It's me."

Hyun Suk looked up at her in surprise. He glanced at the clock on the wall and saw that it was after 11pm. While Hyun Suk was pleasantly surprised with her visit, especially at this late hour, he was also apprehensive of why she had visited so unexpectedly.

"Why are you here? Why today? It isn't Thursday. It's late at night."

Yeon Mee kept her silence. In earlier years, whenever Hyun Suk met Yeon Mee, he was always calm and relaxed. But as time went on, as his love grew for her, yet their family feud became more serious, he couldn't compose himself in front of her. Since then, Hyun Suk always showed a duality—

a duality of stability and anxiousness. It was heart wrenching for Yeon Mee who watched him struggle as he bounced between his two states. And tonight, she could sense the two colliding attitudes in Hyun Suk's eyes. She thought, even after 30 years he hasn't changed. But tonight, although it hurt to see his somber countenance, she thought that even his gloomy expression was lovable. She loved looking at that face, but she knew it wasn't fair to enjoy looking at him so much. She thought, tonight he seems as close to me as he had been thirty years ago.

She said, "I remember the very first time you came to see me in front of my house. You seem the same now, just as shy as you were then."

Hyun Suk smiled at her, trying to understand why she was saying these things.

Again, she spoke, "When you tried to hold my hand on our first date, I didn't refuse because you were so sweet and shy, just like today."

"How can you remember that far back?"

"I remember absolutely every detail."

At this moment, what were they thinking about each other? There were two kinds of smiles between them, barely decipherable at this moment. If Hyun Suk's smile could be decoded, a certain hollowness could be detected whereas Yeon Mee's smile contained less of that sense of loss. Yes, indeed there really was more emptiness in the smile of Hyun Suk than in that of Yeon Mee tonight.

Yeon Mee looked over by his bed and saw that he had placed a bag there.

She asked, "Why are you already packing your bag? You still have several days left here."

"I have too much time on my hands here, nothing to do," he said.

They looked at each other, not speaking for a while.

Hyun Suk asked again, not looking at her,

"Why did you come here? So late? You told me you would come on Thursday."

"I won't be coming on Thursday. Today is the last time we will see each other," she said.

There was deep sadness, a sense of finality, in her voice. He looked slowly up at her, raising his eyebrows in a question. Their eyes met. They held each other's gaze for a long time. Yeon Mee's eyes had reddened. Hyun Suk thought to himself in wonder,

'Why has she come without any notice? Does it mean that she now wants to cut me off entirely, even from her thoughts? From the moment when I first saw her in the hospital, I believed she was devoted to me. I was overcome with joy, but now something in her has changed…oh, I feel so low. And why, oh why has she come tonight? Why so soon? She said she was going to come on Thursday, and it isn't Thursday yet. I wanted to savour those two more nights. That would have been like two whole years for me, looking forward to her coming. I just don't want to lose those two special nights. But here she is now, she's come early, she's taken me by surprise. It's an awful surprise. I feel shaken, devastated. Look at my hands now, they are shaking. And that dreadful pain has suddenly come back into my legs. My whole body feels cold and empty. For the past thirty years I have never stopped thinking of her. For thirty years, for her sake, always dreaming of her, I have never touched another woman. Now it's too late to tell her that. I wish I could have told her, but I can't now, it's just too late. It's just as if I had caught a virus thirty years ago, a virus that took away all my sense of taste and smell. Lately, since I have been seeing her again, thank God, my sense of taste and smell has returned. But now I see, I understand now at last, that I am nothing more than a speck on a piece of paper… Oh, this is all too heavy, I can't bear it. I don't think I can ever get over it now.'

Hyun Suk let out a deep sigh of misery. He turned away from her to hide his tears. And they sat, a profound silence settled between them for a long while. Hyun Suk moved over to his bed and took out a small envelope from under the pillow. He handed it carefully to her.

"Here is the hospital fee, you have been very good to me, you paid for everything."

He added hurriedly, "I know it isn't the full amount, but I'll definitely be able to pay back the rest later."

Yeon Mee didn't want to accept it. She took it from his hand and placed it back under his pillow. Hyun Suk took it out again and went over and put it into her handbag. There was another long and painful silence between them.

After a while, he asked her, "Will you be living in *Choon Chun*?"

"I'm not sure." She said.

"If you live in *Choon Chun* I hope I'll have another chance to see you again. We have never had that chance before. And yet here we are, we have met up again. Really, it's a miracle, isn't it?"

Yeon Mee said nothing for a moment, then spoke,

"Please take good care of your son." For just an instant, her eyes became red again.

"Do you miss him?" Hyun Suk asked.

Yeon Mee tried to say something but found that she couldn't. She gently shook her head, choking back tears. He got up and went over to her.

"You need to go now," he said firmly. He understood that she needed to leave.

"I'd like to hold your hand," he said, softly.

He held out his hand towards her. As he tried to take her hand, Hyun Suk felt something huge pushing against his heart. He told himself that he must now somehow detach himself from her, but he didn't know how to do it. The old saying that love conquered all was so wrong, oh so wrong. He thought, why did I believe in the old saying, true love can conquer all? His thoughts began to become despondent as he thought. I don't like myself. I wish I could cling to her dress and never, never let her go. I wish I could enclose her forever in the safe haven of my heart. In deep sadness he reflected, I have always been steadfast in my love for her. My feelings have never changed in all these years. If they had ever wavered, it might be easier now to let her go. Or if there was any chance, any slight chance that she was utterly broken and devastated right now, perhaps I could have declared my love. But her feelings towards me have shifted, I am sure of that now. I only wish that we could recapture the same old harmony we used to have between us, the same equilibrium. I wish we could relate again as equals. But now I am aware that she has grown away from me. She mixes in a more prestigious social circle than mine. She has risen ever-upward over the years, while I have sunk lower and lower, and it has all been downhill for me. The gap between us has grown too great, I see that now, and I can no longer tell her how much I love her.

She did not take his hand. She turned to her handbag and

took out a handkerchief. Hyun Suk took his hand back. In the end, the two of them couldn't hold hands. They had lost their last chance to hold hands.

Yeon Mee wiped her eyes, tried to smile at him, and said, "Do you understand why I can't hold your hands now? If we hold hands it would be as if the past had never happened between us."

He nodded.

"I really must leave, now. Please take care of yourself."

He smiled at her as she walked backwards away from him, holding his gaze. Then, she was gone. After she left, Hyun Suk's shoulders sank in utter dejection.

Yeon Mee went out the gate of the hospital. Her eye makeup was smudged from her tears. She tried to wipe them dry with the handkerchief. Although she greatly regretted having to say goodbye to Hyun Suk, she felt even more regretful that she was not able to be the mother she should have been to Jeong Soo. She would dearly have loved to have gotten to know him, but she knew above all that her long-term relationship with Sung Jae and his family would not be able to survive that particular truth. After leaving the hospital, Yeon Mee felt that on this occasion she had made the best decision for everyone. A voice behind her called,

"Miss Choo! Miss Choo!"

She turned and saw her father's doctor.

"I must tell you that I am very concerned," he said.

"Is there a problem with my father's results?"

"No, it's not your father, it's the patient in room 506, Mr Yang Hyun Suk. A few days ago, I noticed he was in pain, and so I consulted his past records from the other hospital."

"And?"

The doctor paused, then said, "He is gravely ill."

"Wait… what? How severe is it? Could it be fatal?"

The doctor nodded.

#

Hyun Suk's house.

Jeong Soo was having dinner with his family. He said to his wife,

"Have there been any phone calls from my dad?"

"No."

"Let's wait until after the weekend, and if we haven't heard from him by then, I'll take time off work and go to *Choon Chun* to find him."

Jeong Soo's wife placed her chopsticks slowly on the table. She hesitated, then said,

"There's something I have to tell you. I did get a letter from him. Also, a phone call."

Her husband stared at her in surprise. She continued,

"Your father told me on the phone that when he was writing his letter, he had been drinking too much. He said I couldn't open it, nor show it to you. He told me to destroy it."

"What! Why didn't you tell me?"

"Your father begged me not to." Jeong Soo put his spoon down firmly on the table, and thought, now I am really worried. Why would my father call my wife and ask her not to tell me about this letter? Why would he write a letter in the first place? I don't understand at all.

Suddenly Jeong Soo recalled the look on his father's face as he left home that day.

"Where is that letter?" he asked urgently.

"You can't read it. Your father would be very angry."

"Where is it? You must give it to me right now."

12
The Past

Hyun Suk's Secret Place.

Yeon Mee took out the lunchbox she had prepared for Hyun Suk.

"What's this?" he asked her.

"It's a lunchbox."

"Why is it so big?"

"Do you know what day this coming Saturday will be?"

Hyun Suk stared at her, blankly.

"It's your birthday! Didn't you know? I can't be with you on Saturday, so I came today instead. I'm sorry I'm late today. I was waiting for my mother to go out, then I had to prepare the food. The weather was bad, and the road was quite difficult. That's why I'm late, I'm sorry. The lunch I had planned for us became a dinner instead. You must be hungry."

Hyun Suk was impressed. Outside, there was heavy rain and wind. There was mud everywhere. It had been a long uphill climb for her, up here to his secret place on the mountain. He was surprised and full of admiration for her effort in getting here with that special box. She was wet but didn't care at all and just started to lay out the lunch. How considerate she was! How beautiful she was looking today! Ever since the Jazz Festival, their families had held a grudge towards one other. As he had tried to step back a little from her, Yeon Mee moved even closer to him. He realised that he was falling in love with her, but he thought he should try not to. He must try to control himself because there were so many obstacles in the way of their being together. But then he had begun to think that perhaps the real obstacles were not really family difficulties but had more to do with the ideological split between traditional Korean and Western music. Therefore, surely those obstacles could be overcome with time.

Yeon Mee finished preparing the platter for lunch and brought it to him. He looked long into her eyes, so long that she became embarrassed.

She went looking for a towel to dry her hair. As she was taking it off a hook near the piano, she caught sight of a music score. She asked him if he had written it.

"It's not finished yet," Hyun Suk replied.

"Jazz Lovers," she asked, "Is that the title?"

"Yes, I'm writing it for someone special."

She looked closely at it, then observed,

"Um… the score doesn't seem to be uplifting, contrary to the title. It's rather melancholic. Ah, but there are some beautiful parts in here too. Even the composition is unique, with bossa nova and the tango rhythm! Can I play it now?"

"Not yet."

"Who is it for?" she asked.

Hyun Suk smiled. "Not you, don't expect that! I plan to give it to your father."

She looked surprised. He went on, looking into her eyes,

"If I could somehow meet with your father and give him this score, I think it would be the most powerful statement I could make to show him my feelings of love for you. It would say more than any words could express. My dream is that if your father gives us permission to see each other, then on that day we could play this for him, you on the piano and me on the Haegeum."

Yeon Mee looked at him very seriously. She felt not only a warm breeze on her face but also a dark cloud that came over her. Quietly, she picked up the dish she had prepared and handed him the spoon.

"I have been holding it close to me to keep it warm. Try it."

Hyun Suk leaned back with his hands behind his head and stared at the ceiling. Yeon Mee tried to fathom his mood. He had told her that even if he looked sad sometimes, he was really happy. And when he looked happy, in fact, he was sad. Sometimes, she thought he was a complete mystery to her. One day, she asked him which season was his favourite. He replied it was summer. She then questioned again why summer. He answered that it was because summer was the closest season to autumn. He carried on, further explaining that his life is happy because he could look forward with happy anticipation to the autumn season, when she queried what he meant. So, in the end autumn was his favourite season. Finally, Yeon Mee felt like she was starting to get a better sense of his character.

Yeon Mee went over to the door where she had left another gift for him. She picked up the small package and untied it.

"I have prepared something else for you. Shall I open it?" She opened the gift box with a look of joy.

"It's a miniature Harley Davidson!" he exclaimed.

She nodded, smiling. "Shall I turn it on?" she asked.

She turned on the switch and the little engine roared into

action. Hyun Suk was motionless. This was such a surprise. He didn't expect her to do anything like this for him.

"I saw it in a jazz magazine. It made me think of you. You do like the Harley sound, don't you? Honestly, I can't gauge how much better the Harley engines sound compared to ordinary motorbikes yet. But I still wanted to give this to you."

He was just standing there, gazing at her.

"I don't know why, but I ordered it from overseas for you," she said.

Hyun Suk was thinking about how lovely she was. He took her hand. But suddenly, lightening appeared followed by a loud clap of thunder. Torrential rain began to fall. Hyun Suk went over to the window and looking out, said, "We have to go."

He started to pick up clothes and push them into bags, ready to go. He brought her raincoat over to her.

"But it's raining heavily." Yeon Mee said, "Why don't we wait until it's stopped?"

Hyun Suk went back to the window and looked out.

"No, it's set in. The rain might get even worse later. We have to go."

She didn't reply and just stood there, not wanting to leave. Hyun Suk helped her put on her raincoat. He quickly finished packing the bags, took her hand, and they ran outside together. Hyun Suk had his umbrella in one hand, but it was too fragile and instantly blew inside out.

It was getting dark. They reached the valley, where there should have been a small stone bridge over the stream, but it was covered in water. Hyun Suk tried to make another bridge with some fallen logs and Yeon Mee tried to cross, but she stumbled in the gushing water and fell into the stream. Hyun

Suk helped her out. She was soaking wet. They couldn't go on now. There was no choice but to turn back to his secret place.

Their clothes were sodden. Hyun Suk passed Yeon Mee a towel that was hanging on the wall. She tried to take off her cardigan, facing the wall, but it was made of cotton and it clung to her, and so she turned to him for help. He tried not to look at her wet top clinging to her breasts but saw that she wasn't wearing a bra. He saw that she wasn't shy, but he felt very shy. Yeon Mee rubbed herself dry with her hands, saying, "I'm freezing cold." She was shivering.

He looked around for something, went over behind the piano and fetched a large grain sack which he held up, hiding his face, so she could change. He said, "Why don't you take off your shirt, squeeze the water out, and put it back on? I'll light the fire once you're done."

Yeon Mee's face lit up with a big smile. She thought, he is so sweet and funny holding up that grain sack, when he could just turn himself around and face the wall! I can see that he is modest and shy. His manner is so gentle, he is so innocent. I can't help falling in love with him, right here and now.

Yeon Mee was squeezing out her clothes behind the grain sack. She indicated with her chin that he must lift it up, because he hadn't noticed it was too low. He raised it hastily. All this time, the thunder and lightning continued, and the wind rattled the house. They heard the door smashing, and Yeon Mee huddled close to Hyun Suk. Rain started to pour in through the door, so Hyun Suk passed the grain sack to her and went over to try to close it. He rolled a millstone against it, but it carried on banging, so he added two more weights to put against it. He dusted off his hands and went back to Yeon Mee. He saw that she had let her clothes drop to the floor, and there she stood, naked to the waist, before him. He looked away shyly, but she looked steadily at him, never taking her eyes off him.

When Yeon Mee had first met Hyun Suk, she had noticed his perfect skin and thought how noble and aristocratic he looked. He had a sweet face, beautiful eyes, nose, and lips, and it did not matter to her that he was not wealthy. She had noticed, however, that he was always alone, serious, and introverted. Over time, she had begun to understand why he looked like that. The torment of his mind, she believed, was caused by the clash between traditional Korean and Western music. She had thought that she might be able to calm his spirit and help him with his dilemma in time, with loving care. But soon, she began to realise that she might not be able to help him at all. The reason being that Hyun Suk believed there were too many differences between their families which couldn't be overcome. She started to sense that he didn't want their relationship to develop any further. After some time, she had spoken more directly to him about their relationship, wanting reassurance that he loved her too. Overcoming her pride and reticence, she had found that she was becoming impatient and suspicious that he might never change. But she wanted to make love with him. She didn't want to give up on him. She had begun to feel that he might not return his love for her, and it was beginning to break her heart. She became even more determined to win him over.

Hyun Suk picked up her clothes and passed them to her, holding up the grain sack again as a screen. She just stood there, quite still, looking at the ground, feeling more and more sad and rejected. She said,

"Hyun Suk, this is the fourth time it's happened now, and

you are still refusing me? You said the music score was for my father. But is it really? Is there someone else in your life? And why did you tell me all about your brother's girlfriend coming to your parents' home to make kimchi? Why don't you take me to your parents' house too so I can make kimchi for them? Why do you go on refusing me? You know, ever since you told me that story, I have been practising making many kinds of kimchi too."

13

Hyun Suk, his mother, and brother were sitting in the courtyard making Haegeums. His father was inside the house, testing the quality of the strings on the finished products. Hyun Suk was using an electric saw to cut the small pieces of wood needed for the Haegeums and his mother was painting the finished products. His brother was chopping up the larger pieces of wood that would be used to make the instruments.

The town councillor came into the courtyard and greeted them all. He asked to speak to the father. Yong Ju appeared at the sliding door of the inside room. Suspecting that the town councillor had sided with the mayor, he reluctantly greeted the town councillor and invited him in.

"Yong Ju, the mayor decided to sign to change the Haegeum school into a Piano school tomorrow."

Yong Ju knew this was coming so he wasn't surprised, just very disappointed.

The town councillor went on, "Mr. Choo has given a lot of money to the city council for the scholarship."

"I don't understand," said Yong Ju, "I don't know how much money Mr Choo has donated to the city council, but how could they plan to build a piano school on a land that was meant for a Haegeum school just because of his donation?"

The town councillor looked ashamed and embarrassed to answer these questions to the father of Hyun Suk. He said,

"I'm sorry, but other town representatives have also supported the Piano School. Mr Choo has offered free lessons to every new student to give them the opportunity to decide if they want to go ahead with their piano studies."

Yong Ju said, bitterly,

"Mr Choo is only interested in making money. Some free lessons are nothing! They will all end up having to pay."

They both remained silent a moment.

The town councillor said, "Please give my regards to the Haegeum teacher and apologise to him about the Piano School."

There was another matter that he wanted to discuss with Yong Ju, but he was hesitant about whether or not to raise it now. However, he said quietly,

"I want to talk to you about Hyun Suk."

"What about him?" asked his father.

"I don't know if he is telling you what he's been doing."

"What other problem is there now?"

"Well, a couple of days ago, I was looking at the student registration list for the Piano School, and his name was on it. Like I've said before, this is a worry, seeing he is from a traditional Korean family devoted to the Haegeum. I don't understand why he is doing this. I know there is an important Haegeum exam coming up in a few weeks. There's a lot of competition and a very high standard in order to pass. Despite this, so many parents are still supporting their children in their Haegeum studies. But they may be influenced by seeing Hyun Suk going over to the piano. Last year, the standard of his Haegeum playing dropped, and this year is his last chance. He's by far the best provincial player at the moment. You've made him number one and our town is proud of him. But if his skill on the Haegeum continues to fall, people will stop donating towards Haegeum production and we will never be able to build our Haegeum School." The town councillor looked despondent.

Yong Ju felt dismayed at the sudden change in the councillor's attitude towards the Haegeum. The town councillor went on to say that craftsmen would disappear from the town and that already many teenagers were losing interest in traditional music. "I don't expect much from them anymore." There was silence between them.

The town councillor came out from the sliding door. He looked across at Hyun Suk with annoyance as he crossed the courtyard and left.

When he was gone, Yong Ju kicked open the sliding door viciously, and barefooted, ran across to Hyun Suk. He was in a rage and was ready to hit his son. His wife raised her hand to her mouth in shock. Hyun Meen ran over to try to stop his father from attacking his brother, but his father pushed him aside and landed a punch squarely in Hyun Suk's face. Hyun Suk fell backwards. In rage and disappointment, Yong Ju shouted,

"Why have you done that? Why have you applied to the Piano School again?" Hyun Suk's nose was bleeding all over his mouth. Yong Ju stormed over to the shed and back out with a large stick the size of a baseball bat. This time, his wife threw herself at him desperately and held on to his left leg, while Hyun Meen grabbed his arms to stop him assaulting his brother again.

"Put that down," cried his wife, "you are going too far."

With his arms held back, Yong Ju still managed to kick Hyun Suk on his side and stomp on his back with his right leg.

Hyun Suk's mother started to scream. Hyun Meen wrestled the bat from his father, who then raised his fist to punch Hyun Suk yet again. He was not strong enough to restrain him, and Yong Ju managed to punch Hyun Suk continuously. Hyun Suk's mother ran over to the fence to call to the neighbour, Mr Kim, for help.

Mr Kim ran barefoot out from his house across his courtyard to see what was happening. He jumped over the wall and came running. Between them, he managed to subdue Yong Ju, who remained staring at his son in fury, eyes blazing. All of them were splattered with blood.

In agony, Yong Ju cried,

"You never stop crushing me! Don't you know that I have spent my whole life working for your future, ever since you were a child? Your brother and I were always selling second-hand goods at stalls to support your Haegeum education! Must I bow down to you now? I have begged you over and over not to register at that Piano School, and still, you defy me."

Yong Ju lunged towards Hyun Suk, trying to punch him again. This time, Mr Kim managed to stop him. Then, they heard a voice at breaking point crying out,

"Stop that! Just stop it, stop it at once!"

It was Hyun Meen. This was the first time their parents had ever heard their son cry out like that. They stood stunned, staring at him.

Hyun Meen shouted, "Dad, can't you see that your two little boys are grown men now! You just can't do this. You can't go on treating us like this!"

His father flinched. Fury overtook him again,

"You little shits!" he snarled.

"Don't talk to us like that!" cried Hyun Meen.

76

Their father paused, surprised. He had had disobedient behaviour from Hyun Meen from time to time, but never anything like this. It was unbelievable.

Hyun Meen cried,

"You are wrong to say Hyun Suk registered at the Piano School. He doesn't know anything about it! It was me who registered him!"

His parents stared at him in astonishment. Hyun Suk, huddled on the ground, tried to turn over and focus his swollen eyes on his brother, and the whole story of their childhood flashed across his mind as he lay there...

Ever since they were very young, the two brothers had made and played Haegeums together. It had been an entirely Haegeum-focused family. Their father had expected them to be the finest players of the future. However, as they reached puberty, the two boys came under the influence of western culture. They grew to like and admire it, and this had always been the reason for their father's continued violence towards them. During one such episode, Hyun Meen had decided that he wasn't really talented on the Haegeum and had given it up. He had decided instead to just become a maker of Haegeums. Yong Ju had then begun to focus on Hyun Suk, intending on making him into the finest player, and this became his abiding obsession. He became more and more driven by ambition, and this led to more violence against his son, and constant beatings with a stick. In the end, Yong Ju had caused permanent damage to Hyun Suk's knee cartilage which required an operation. From then on, Hyun Suk always walked with a limp. The result of all this violence was that Hyun Suk no longer cared anymore about the Haegeum instrument nor about the family tradition. Instead, he turned his attention to the piano and western jazz in particular. He grew to love it very much. Then, Yeon Mee and her father, the piano teacher, had come into his life when they moved into his town. His ambition then soared to great heights with jazz. By chance, one day, he had tried to play jazz on the Haegeum, and to his surprise, he found that it made an amazing sound. The Haegeum didn't have to be played only in the traditional way at all! Jazz sounded very powerful and exciting when played on the Haegeum, especially when accompanied by the piano. The only stumbling block in his life at that point was the hostile attitude of his father. Hyun Suk had tried to share his feelings of pain and loneliness with his brother, but Hyun Meen had rejected him, always choosing to support their father until this moment, lying here on the ground, bashed up once again by their father. Here was his brother, speaking out at last in support of him. Hyun Meen had even applied to the Piano School on his behalf! It was almost unbelievable. A feeling of warmth flooded into Hyun Suk's heart, of great gratitude towards his brother. It moved him very deeply.

Hyun Meen was talking again to Yong Ju,

"I'm telling you truthfully, we don't even know very much about the family business, or how important it is. Dad, are we really working for the family business? No, we are not. We are working for you. We have always worked for you, our father. And you in turn worked for your own father, our grandfather, because he had a dream of having a Haegeum School in this town. He couldn't fulfil his dream, so you have tried to do it for him. You have always worked for him, not for us. Dad, just as you did for your father, we have done everything for you. We have worked solely for you."

Their father fell silent, overcome. Hyun Meen carried on

speaking, sadly,

"Do you now understand what I mean? Please give us the chance at last to make our own choices in life. Please understand this between father and son. You have been too selfish, thinking only about yourself. Try to think about us and our needs."

Yong Ju seemed to be listening, understanding a little at last. He looked down. His son went on,

"A long time ago, Hyun Suk told me that the most difficult experience he has ever faced in his life was having to pretend to love something that he didn't love at all. That was Korean traditional music. And after, he told me there is something even harder than that to bear, and that is loving something that he's not able to get close to. For him, that is jazz."

Yong Ju stared at his son, speechless.

Hyun Meen spoke again,

"When Hyun Suk told me that, I understood him. But I felt I couldn't admit it, and that I must support you, our father, and I pretended I didn't understand him."

Tears came into Hyun Suk's eyes when he heard this. His brother continued,

"Dad, surely you feel sorry for him. Surely you understand now. Remember what you did to his leg? That was the biggest mistake of your life, but Hyun Suk never held a grudge against you. If I were a father and had a son, I wouldn't do what you did to him. There can't be another parent in the world like you."

Yong Ju felt anger rising up in him again. His face burned and he began to shake.

"You son of a bitch!" he cried. He ran towards Hyun Meen to attack him, but the neighbour held him back. Yong Ju pointed in rage at Hyun Suk and shouted,

"Under no circumstances will you quit the Haegeum! You will keep going with it!"

He pointed towards Hyun Meen, and hissed at him,

"And you, you have to stay making Haegeums forever!"

He pointed back at Hyun Suk, shouting,

"If you play the piano and Western music on the Haegeum, you can get out of my house!"

He pointed again at Hyun Meen,

"You can cancel your registration to the Piano School right now!"

Hyun Meen responded firmly,

"No, I can't!"

Yong Ju's anger grew even more, and he managed to push the neighbour out of the way. He grabbed the Haegeum and bashed it. He headed towards Hyun Meen, glaring ferociously. Suddenly, he lost his balance, and fainted, collapsing on the ground. His wife rushed over and knelt beside him. The neighbour tried to revive him, but he had fallen unconscious. Hyun Meen tried to carry his father on his back but couldn't because his father was so heavy. The neighbour carried Yong Ju on his back instead. His wife and Hyun Meen followed him out the gate. Hyun Suk watched them disappear out of sight…

14

The Present

A couple of days before, when Yeon Mee was going to the hospital, she had promised herself that she would not be broken-hearted about having to say farewell to Hyun Suk. However, her intentions were overturned by the shock of the news she had received from the doctor. Hearing news of colon cancer made her break the promise she had made to Sung Jae: that she would never meet up with Hyun Suk or disappoint his family again. She knew that this would break Sung Jae's heart. The truth was that she did indeed love Sung Jae, and there was no doubt that she would end up marrying him. She had made up her mind about that long ago. Nevertheless, her feelings of compassion towards Hyun Suk at his plight pulled her back again.

Yeon Mee was standing at the door of Hyun Suk's hospital room. The door was ajar. She peeped around it and saw him on the bed. He wasn't lying down but was kneeling with his head buried in the pillow, as if he was trying to hide himself away from the world. Yeon Mee silently opened the door further and came in. She sat down carefully near the door and watched him. Eventually she said,

"It's me. I'm here again."

Hyun Suk lifted his head in surprise to look at her.

Yeon Mee's voice was stern and cold,

"Can you guess why I've come again? I want to ask you about something. Perhaps I shouldn't, but…"

He looked at her questioningly, and she went on,

"Why did you do such a silly thing? Why do I now think you're stupid?"

He stared at her in shock. Why was she being so cruel?

"Even if your life is dreary and you are sick and tired, you shouldn't have behaved like that. What about your family? Frankly, I hadn't realised that you were irresponsible."

Hyun Suk looked away. For quite a while, there was silence in the room.

"Hi Grandad!"

A small girl's voice was heard at the door. In she came, followed by Hyun Suk's son Jeong Soo and his wife. Yeon Mee could no longer ask Hyun Suk for the answers she wanted. Her eyes met Jeong Soo, and she knew from the moment he entered the room that she was looking into the eyes of her own son. Both she and Hyun Suk were taken by surprise. This visit was entirely unexpected. They looked at each other and a pact of secrecy passed between them. Yeon Mee slowly rose to her feet, a sign of respect. She couldn't leave quickly; she must be courteous. She went over to the table, rummaged in her bag, and put on her scarf to get ready to go, telling herself to remain calm and composed.

Jeong Soo's wife's face was full of sorrow. She approached Hyun Suk, and said,

"Hello Father. What's happening? Are you okay?"

Jeong Soo was upset. He wondered who this woman was. He walked over to his father's bed, looked down at him, took a deep breath, and sighed, not sure what to say to him at this moment. Son and father's eyes met briefly, then both looked away. Jeong Soo caught sight of Yeon Mee and saw that her eyes were glistening with tears. And yet, there was also joy in her look, and he couldn't make out the meaning of this joy. There was no mathematical equation to explain this paradox of human emotion, from which nothing can be added or taken away.

Jeong Soo looked at Yeon Mee again. He wondered why she was observing him with such intensity. Hyun Suk noticed too and interrupted this train of thought asking,

"How did you know I was here?"

Jeong Soo's attention moved from Yeon Mee back to his father. Yeon Mee was even taking an interest in the shape of the back of his head.

Then pulling herself together, she turned to Hyun Suk and said, "It was lovely to meet you, Mr Yang Hyun Suk. Let's talk again later. Now is the time for you to be with your family."

Hyun Suk bowed, formally saying, "Let's talk again later."

And then, Yeon Mee left the room.

15

The Past

The Haegeum Practice Room.

Hyun Suk opened the door to the classroom. All the students looked up at him. The Haegeum teacher, Hyo Jun, said with a sigh,

"Excuse me, Hyun Suk, why don't you say sorry for being so late?"

Hyun Suk stood and bowed to everyone as an apology.

"Do you know what day it is today?" asked Hyo Jun.

"Yes, I know."

"Then you know that the head of Cultural Education is coming?"

"Yes, I know."

"Therefore, today is the most important day of your life."

"Yes, I know."

"You knew, then why are you late?"

"I'm sorry. I had to go to the hospital with my father."

At that juncture, there was an announcement saying the head of Cultural Education had arrived. Hyo Jun straightened his collar and shirt and went out to meet him.

The students were seated in a row outside the examination room. Each had a number attached to his or her shirt. Hyun Suk was among them. The sound of the Haegeum could be heard from inside the room. Then a voice called 'Number 12, Yang Hyun Suk!'

He went into the room holding his Haegeum. He approached the three examiners and the head of cultural education. Hyun Suk pulled out a seat, bowed, and told them his name.

"What are you going to play?" he was asked by an assistant examiner.

"*Bita Culture.*"

The assistant examiner nodded. Hyun Suk adjusted the Haegeum on his knees, and began to play...

His initial technique was good, which took them by surprise. While they were taking notes, suddenly alert, they began to watch him closely. They looked at each other in surprise, satisfied with what they were hearing. However, after a minute and thirty seconds of him playing, a look of suspicion began to come over their faces. They felt confused by this new development. Why was he playing like this? *Bita Culture* was a traditional Korean piece of music. However, Hyun Suk was playing an unfamiliar arrangement. He was infusing it with a jazz technique, unheard of until then. One of the assistant examiners asked, disconcerted, "What are you doing?"

Hyun Suk looked up but kept on playing.

"Excuse me, student, but why are you playing like that?" asked another examiner.

Hyun Suk ignored him, closed his eyes, and continued playing as before, deeply involved in his music.

One of the examiners repeated his question, louder,

"Would you please stop playing?"

Hyun Suk stopped playing.

"Excuse me, Mr Yang," asked the other examiner, "will

you please tell us exactly what style of music you are playing?"

"It's *Bita Culture*," answered Hyun Suk.

"Why are you playing it like that? I don't understand," he said sternly.

"*Bita Culture* is a versatile piece and free expression is possible. That's why I was playing it like that. Is there a problem with this?"

"Yes, we understand the piece can be adapted. However, the style you are adopting is western, foreign to us, and not at all Korean." declared the examiner.

Hyun Suk said, confidently,

"I know that there is no law forbidding western-style music."

The head examiner raised his voice in a critical tone,

"Do you understand how important this examination is, young man? You play skilfully, but why are you being so stubborn?"

Hyun Suk paused, took a deep breath,

"I do not mean to be stubborn. I have been playing for over twenty years. It has taken me twenty years of playing to discover the expressive power of the Haegeum. The Haegeum played traditionally is one of the best sounds in the world of stringed instruments. I understand that, but it is a pity to confine it only to the traditional mode. Why not experiment combining it with other genres to enrich its power and range? Jazz played on the Haegeum is inspiring! That's what I wanted to demonstrate to you today."

All three examiners and the head of cultural education sat there, stunned.

The head examiner asked him, "Last year when you took

the exam, you weren't playing like that. If you get lower than average marks this time, you will miss the chance for entry into the finals. Why try a risky experiment on a day like this?"

Hyun Suk replied,

"When I sat the exam last year, I had no idea that the Haegeum could make such a marvellous sound."

The head examiner asked,

"I think you would have many opportunities elsewhere to try mixing genres, but why on such an important day as this?"

"My goal is not simply to pass the iconic Korean Haegeum tradition onto future generations, but it also is to delve into other genres, using the Haegeum, and to find peace of mind in developing a new art form. Many people don't understand my technique, but you have great experience and depth of knowledge about the Haegeum so I thought you might appreciate a new style of playing."

All the examiners looked at one another, and silence fell in the room.

The head examiner asked,

"What are you going to play next?"

"*Fly Me to the Moon*."

"What kind of music is that?"

"It was composed by Bart Howard from America. Many jazz musicians enjoy playing this song."

"Your first piece was Korean traditional music combined with western-style. Your second selection is pure western jazz?"

"Yes, but if you don't want to hear it, I will leave."

Puzzled, the head examiner looked at the others. He was thinking for a moment whether he should request him to leave or just hear him play. All the others watched his face for the lead.

"Okay, go ahead," he said.

Hyun Suk started to play. A lot of noise was coming from outside the room. Many students had crowded to the window along with the Haegeum teacher, Hyo Jun, listening in shock. Hyo Jun was holding back his anger. He put his hands to his head, clutching his hair in frustration.

A year ago, when Hyun Suk had listened to *Fly Me to the Moon* on the radio being played by Wes Montgomery (American jazz guitarist) on the guitar, he had fallen in love with it. He had tried to write it down, but he had bought the whole record album instead. He started to play it on the Haegeum and now, it had become one of his favourite pieces.

Halfway through his performance, to the great surprise of the examiners, Hyun Suk changed the timing to an irregular tempo. Hyun Suk had played *Bita Culture* in slow tempo, and now *Fly Me to the Moon* was being played very fast with a high degree of skill. They had never heard anything like it before! Hyun Suk was actually humming along with the melody. He was playing the instrument with his bow and drumming on it simultaneously. The examiners became even more surprised. His style was entirely harmonious. He was playing a beautiful song, but in fact, his mood was quite the gloomy. Hyun Suk's time was up. The head examiner and the other three examiners remained silent for a while. The judges all thought he was crazy, but on the other hand, they could see he was highly talented and an excellent Haegeum player. However, they didn't share that second part of the thought with him at all. Their faces remained blank.

"You can go now," said the head examiner.

Hyun Suk remained seated and said, "I do understand that

my playing doesn't fit the traditional Haegeum form. But I don't think I have broken any rules playing Western music. I have been honest about that today." He bowed, took his Haegeum and went towards the door. But as he left, the head examiner asked Hyun Suk, "When the Haegeum is played, normally five fingers are used. You used four. Why?"

"My father taught me that when you use four fingers to hold the bow, you can feel the weight better and it helps you to play more skilfully. It creates a better sound."

They just stared at him.

When Hyun Suk went out and closed the door, Hyo Jun struck him across the face. Hyun Suk fell back against the wall. Hyo Jun stopped punching him as the door opened again, and Number 13 was announced.

Hyun Suk left the exam and went for a walk alone. He understood why his father's face kept coming back to him. He felt sorry for him because his father was suffering from a heart condition and Hyun Suk had caused him much distress. However, he knew he had made the right choice. Nevertheless, he couldn't avoid feeling afraid of what his father would say when he heard about the events of today. He took his bicycle and set off for home, but then took a detour instead.

Later that afternoon, Hyun Suk noticed, coming home, that the gate was open, and his father and the Haegeum teacher were standing there. He thought he had better turn around, to avoid a confrontation. He decided to go up a nearby hill, so he could look down and discern their mood.

From the hill he could see his mother was hovering by the gate, looking anxious. He could also see his father sitting down, a rod in his hand, and a carafe of drink beside him. His brother, dressed in a suit, with his girlfriend beside him, was at the rear of the courtyard. He wondered why they were waiting there, but quickly he realised that Hyun Meen had brought his girlfriend, hoping to avert an outburst of rage from his father. Although he was thankful that his brother brought his girlfriend to prevent their father from creating a scene, Hyun Suk couldn't be sure that that would stop him. Hyun Suk didn't want to embarrass her with a scene, so he waited till she had left. He wanted to protect her.

That night.

Hyun Suk staggered in the gate at midnight, quite drunk. He saw straight away that his father was still waiting up for him, sitting exactly as he had been many hours before. Hyun Suk retreated back from the gate.

"Just stop there!" Yong Ju said firmly,

Hyun Suk paused, wondering what to do.

"Are you completely drunk? I've never seen you like that before. Drunk people usually tell the truth. I'm drunk, and so are you. So why don't we tell each other the truth?"

Hyun Suk turned, staggering. Yong Ju said,

"I have one question for you. I understand why your marks dropped in the Haegeum exam last year. Your ability wasn't up to scratch. That's true, isn't it?"

Hyun Suk said nothing.

"You have practised for more than a year now. You would have done much better than your exam last year. You already knew too well that it would set you up for failure. Why have you done that? Why? Just tell me the truth."

Hyun Suk still said nothing.

"Feeling rebellious toward me, is that why?"

Still no reply.

"Please answer me."

Again, silence.

"Do you really not want to play our traditional music?"

Hyun Suk didn't reply. His head was hanging down, and he was staggering on his feet. His father went on,

"Okay then, if you really don't want to play the Haegeum and our traditional music then I will stop forcing you."

Hyun Suk raised his head in surprise.

"I'm asking you once again, do you truly not love playing the Haegeum?"

Finally, Hyun Suk spoke up.

"It's not that. I do love playing the Haegeum, but I don't want to only play traditional music on it." His father looked at him, nonplussed. Hyun Suk spoke again,

"You know, Father, you always told me that when I played the Haegeum it was not simply dexterity with the hand, but that it should come from the heart. That is what you told me. I never understood what you meant by that, until I came across jazz."

His father just stared at him.

"Whenever I played our traditional music, I could barely feel anything at all; not love, beauty, or sadness. It seemed devoid of feeling. But I found that Western music isn't like that at all, especially jazz. After playing jazz, even for a few moments, I could already feel so much love. When I play jazz, it seems that its melody penetrates my heart it and becomes so real that it makes me happy. I'm sorry. You may not like my answer." His speech was slurred.

Yong Ju poured alcohol from his jar into his glass. He

took a large gulp, walked inside the house, and put it on the wooden floor.

"Come over here, sit down and have a drink with me."

Hyun Suk had never before heard his father speak like that to him. He was suspicious of his soft tone. He felt a kind of love for his father for the first time ever. He staggered over the step near his father, took off his shoes, tripped on the wooden deck, then fell down on his knees. His father handed him a glass. Hyun Suk took it and held it out for his father to pour him a drink.

Early the next morning, Hyun Suk awoke. He opened his eyes and looked around. His father wasn't there. He could see only the large alcohol bottles and empty glasses. He could hardly believe that he had been drinking with his father last night. He thought that yesterday, after the exam, he would definitely have brought on another storm from his father. This storm was always filled with heavy thunder and lighting and a lot of anguish. However, it hadn't been like that. There was no storm, but rather, a peaceful sunny day. He never knew what was coming next. Perhaps the sunny day was just a mirage. But this sunny day seemed to be melting the iceberg. Hyun Suk watched the sunrise over the mountains. It was like a gift, granting him happiness in his life at last. He stood up and looked into Yong Ju's room. Outside were his father's shoes. He thought he was asleep in there, then wondered again if there hadn't actually been a storm yesterday. He could hardly believe it. He had told his father that he would never give up Western music, and he was still alive this morning! This must be the most beautiful morning ever.

The next day.

Before dawn, Hyun Suk was climbing the mountain, heading to his secret place where he kept his piano. Suddenly, he felt that both his piano and jazz music were no longer a burden weighing him down. He felt light and free. Today, so different from all other days, his fingers played better than ever, the most beautiful melody and song. He stayed there all day long from sunrise to sunset.

Darkness had crept up around him in his secret place. When Hyun Suk was about to leave, there was a knock on the door. It had to be Yeon Mee. Why was she coming so late? He looked through the small window near the door and saw that it was indeed her. He opened the door. There she stood. She smiled at him briefly then became serious. He couldn't read her mind. Suddenly, she leant her head against his chest.

"What's the matter?" he asked.

She took a step back and turned her gaze toward the distant mountains. Anxiously, she paced the ground.

"What is the matter, tell me?"

"What can I say? What can we do?" she said.

"Just tell me. What's going on?" he asked again.

"I'm pregnant."

16
The Present

It was as if Yeon Mee's words had stricken Sung Jae's heart with a stone. He was left gasping for air. He asked her,

"Why do you want to postpone meeting my family again?"

She didn't reply.

"Is it because of that man?" his voice sounded strained.

Yeon Mee replied in a thin voice,

"Yes. I have to stay with him a little longer."

Sung Jae felt devastated.

About a week ago, she had told him that nothing had changed between them. "My intentions towards Hyun Suk are innocent. I knew him long ago, and I feel sympathy and goodwill towards him. I thought my duty to him was completely over. To be honest, I thought there was some love left in me. But I couldn't continue this love even if a little was still there." She had said…

Suddenly, Sung Jae felt anger rising in him. He controlled himself with great effort, and only his eyes betrayed him.

He stopped the car and opened the door. It was too stuffy. He pulled at his collar to loosen it.

She said, "I thought the pain in his heart was minimal. Later, I discovered his full circumstances, and his pain is actually extreme."

Sung Jae replied angrily,

"Your reason is just that he has more pain than before. Is that all?"

He went on,

"If that is your only reason, think about the pain and hurt that I am feeling. Think of me, my pain is far worse than his."

Tears were welling up in Yeon Mee's eyes. She wanted to say something to him, but she couldn't. Her lips were trembling.

After a minute she said, "Listen to me, Sung Jae. I have one secret."

He looked at her fearfully, waiting.

"Sung Jae, I have to tell you. I have a son."

Sung Jae looked at her in disbelief, but he kept his silence.

"Sadly, I had never seen my son's face. I had never met him before."

Sung Jae's face lost its anger after hearing the tragedy of her story. He asked,

"Between you and that man?"

Yeon Mee stayed silent a while, then nodded.

"My son never found out who I was. He has only seen me once in the hospital room with his father. This was the first time I had ever seen his face. And when I saw him, I could see that he had had a very hard life. He looked bereft, so sad and insecure, I felt he needed love. I wished I could do something for him." She started crying. Trying to compose herself, she went on,

"So that was the main reason. But I have another reason. I have found out that Hyun Suk is dying."

Sung Jae looked hard at her.

"Try to understand how I feel! I saw my son's face for the

first time in my life. I'm so very sorry, Sung Jae, but I can't be with you, not for a short while yet. Hyun Suk promised he would have an operation to remove the cancer, then a couple of days ago he changed his mind and said he didn't want to go through with it. He wanted to die. Then he changed his mind again and said he wanted to live. Sung Jae, please just wait. Be patient with me, until the operation is over."

Sung Jae was silent. He thought to himself. He wanted to say that Hyun Suk and Yeon Mee's situation was a separate issue from his family's affairs and ask if it was still necessary for her to hold off on meeting his family. But he didn't ask. That's because he knew if there was a possibility that she still viewed Hyun Suk as her lover, that question would make her uncomfortable. On the other hand, if she thought that it wouldn't be polite to meet his family whilst being involved with Hyun Suk, he would also have to respect that. Sung Jae let out a great sigh.

#

Hyun Suk lay on the surgical bed. He was being moved into the operating theatre. He went through the doors, which shut behind him. Through glass screens, his son, daughter-in-law and granddaughter were all standing there watching him. Yeon Mee was standing at some distance from them. Jeong Soo looked across at her, hesitated, then walked towards her. She was looking down at the floor.

"Can I talk with you?" he asked.

She looked up into his face, and for a moment Jeong Soo felt at a loss for words. Then he said, "First, I appreciate your help. You cared for my father while he was in here. The senior manager told me."

Jeong Soo thanked her without any warmth. He looked depressed. He talked to her again,

"I heard you paid for his stay here and supported him over his operation. You also arranged for an expert surgeon to operate on my father. I have no words to express my thanks to you. But I don't understand why you did all that for him. It was my place to do all that. How do you know my father so well? And…"

Yeon Mee cut in on him, saying,

"A long time ago, your father was very good to my father, and I remember that fact, so I wanted to oblige myself by helping your father. I'm sorry I failed to contact you. Your father didn't want that. Maybe ask your father for more details after his operation."

Yeon Mee spoke confidently. Even though she wasn't telling the truth, it all came out naturally somehow. Maybe she had already had time to think through what she would say in this situation. In her heart however, she was in the depths of misery. She looked out the window, thinking, this is the first conversation I have ever had with my son. And it is all lies. It felt as if she was reading from a script. This wasn't real life, just fiction.

17
The Past

Civil Engineers were working on the construction of the Piano School. Foundation posts were all in place. Out in front, a group of people were talking together. Mr Choo was talking with the mayor. Others were clustered behind them. Further away from the construction site was a large tree where sacks of rice were stacked. Hyun Suk's father, Yong Ju, was hovering behind the sacks, getting angrier and angrier as he watched the progress of the Piano School. He wanted to come and see it for himself, remembering that this was the very site that had been intended for his Haegeum School. He couldn't accept that his dream had been shattered. He had watched the mayor and Mr Choo smiling in agreement, he had been given no option, and he had no opportunity to put up any resistance. He felt his legs giving way under him. He sank down to the ground in despair.

#

Yong Ju's House.

The Haegeum teacher, Hyo Jun, was grumbling to Yong Ju,

"Well, Yong Ju, we might as well now work as farmers. There's no one left who calls this town the Haegeum Town.

No one acknowledges that we have kept our traditional music and instruments alive. If only your son could pass this final examination, then at least our town could maintain some pride in itself. I'm really sorry, Yong Ju, that I failed to teach Hyun Suk successfully."

Yong Ju finished drinking the last shot from his glass and passed it to Hyo Jun, pouring him another one. Hyo Jun drank it then put it down on the table.

"So, Yong Ju, how do you think we can convince Hyun Suk about his future?"

"You know, Hyo Jun, early this morning the head examiner sent me a letter."

Hyo Jun raised his eyebrows in surprise. What was this all about?

Yong Ju went on, "The head examiner informed me that Hyun Suk had failed the examination, but nevertheless he was given an above-average mark. He said he hoped Hyun Suk would do better next year. If he hadn't been given the above-average mark, he would have lost the opportunity forever. I didn't expect another chance. We are lucky."

Hyo Jun looked amazed, "Do you mean to say that the head examiner actually wrote that in a letter?"

"Yes, it's a letter of acknowledgement." Yong Ju said relieved yet bitter, gulping down another drink.

"Do you know what this means?" Hyo Jun continued, "I didn't expect a letter of acknowledgement. I've never heard of such a letter being sent to a student whose playing is going downhill. Not only that, but the finalists have also already been announced, and the examination period is over. Hyun Suk played Western music that day, yet he was still given an above-average mark, isn't that surprising?"

Yong Ju remained silent. Hyo Jun continued,

"If he hadn't played Western music, he would have passed the examination with flying colours."

Yong Ju nodded silently in agreement.

"One more thing I must say, Yong Ju. On that day, when Hyun Suk had finished playing and was leaving the room, the head examiner asked him why he played with only four fingers. Guess what his reply was."

Yong Ju had been looking down but looked up at Hyo Jun. Hyo Jun went on, "Hyun Suk said that his father had drilled into him that technique. When I heard him say that I detected in his voice some pride towards you. I have an idea, Yong Ju. I think we have no choice if we want to make Hyun Suk into a fine Haegeum player. We need to give him some encouragement, warmth, and love for the next year. The rest of our lives depends on him."

#

Yong Ju was staggering down the road, quite drunk, when he suddenly noticed Mr Choo, the mayor and his three assistants walking along, chatting together. They saw him coming. They all stopped. Yong Ju remained still on the narrow road, but the others carried on walking past him. The mayor looked distinctly uncomfortable. Suddenly, without warning, Yong Ju spat right into his face. It landed in his right eye. Mr Choo and the assistants were shocked at this outrageous behaviour. The assistants became angry, and gave Yong Ju a shove, pushing him backwards. When they were about to do it again, the mayor, who had been walking away, urged them to stop, saying, "Come on, leave this man alone, don't bother with him. Let's just move on."

They were moving on, but once again Yong Ju spat at them, and this time it landed right in Mr Choo's face. At this provocation, they all became wild with anger. The youngest assistant, only nineteen or twenty, burst out to confront Yong Ju, "You've always been unreasonable and rude. When you drink you act even more like a stray dog! I can't believe that your sons are so calm with a father like you, behaving like a wild animal."

There was rage in Yong Ju's eyes. He looked around for something, picked up a stone, and lurched towards the young assistant. The two assistants reacted quickly and grabbed the stone from his hand, threw it away, restraining him by holding his hands behind his back and marching him over to a ditch. Yong Ju slipped on the edge of the ditch, and fell into the water, got up, then fell again, time after time…

Hyun Suk's House.

Hyun Suk's mother came into his room without knocking. She stood looking at him, silently, looking very pale. He had never seen her with such a pale face. He wondered why. Finally, she spoke, calmly, "Son, what's the rumour going around? People are talking about you and Mr Choo's daughter. They saw you and Mr Choo's daughter at the maternity hospital. What's it all about?"

Hyun Suk was shocked. He couldn't answer. He just stared at his mother.

"Who told you that?" he asked her, perplexed.

His mother then realised that the rumour must be true. Then, she became angry and hurt.

"Son, is it true that Mr Choo's daughter is pregnant with

your baby?"

Hyun Suk didn't reply, avoiding her eyes. He couldn't understand how this could be. He lived here in *Choon Chun*, and the maternity hospital was three hundred kilometres away in an entirely different district...

Yeon Mee's House.

Mr Choo slapped Yeon Mee right across the face. She fell back against the wall. Her father lifted her up and slapped her in the face again, sending splatters of blood on to the wall. Her lips and nose were bleeding. He then pulled her into her room and locked the door. Her mother was crying outside, unable to get in. He didn't hear his wife calling, he was in such a rage. He pulled his daughter's hair and dragged her across the floor. He then threw her down on her belly deliberately, losing all self-control. He yelled,

"Why did you do that? I have always taught you to live decently and nobly. You are not a grown woman yet, and you have gone and done that?"

Yeon Mee's mother pushed the piano, its legs on casters, against the door to force it open. She ran towards her daughter, distraught, and embraced her. She was upset to find so much blood from her nose and her lip badly cut. How could her husband do such a terrible thing to their daughter? And yet, she understood why he had lost temper. She also disapproved of the relationship between her daughter and Hyun Suk.

Hyun Suk's House.

Yong Ju opened the gate to his house. He was drunk and swaying. He went over to the small well and cupped his hands under the cold water. Just then, Hyun Suk looked out from his room and saw his father staggering in front of him.

His mother looked out from her room at that moment and saw her husband and son by the well. Her face clouded over. Perhaps she was taking on Hyun Suk's guilt even though she had never done anything wrong herself. Yong Ju looked at his son kneeling before him and wondered why. He looked from his son to his wife.

"What are you doing here?" he asked in a slurred voice.

"Father, I have to tell you something."

After a period of silence, he spoke.

"You know I told you a while ago that if you didn't let me play Western music on the Haegeum I would stop playing the Haegeum altogether? It was inappropriate of me to say that. I am sorry I said that."

He continued, "Now I've changed my mind. I will try my best to play traditional music on the Haegeum and pass the exam as you wish. I will try my best to carry on with the traditional family business making Haegeums."

His father raised his eyebrows, silently.

"So, I'll stop playing the piano," said Hyun Suk, "and I'll completely give up playing Western music."

"I don't understand you," said his father, "what is all this?"

"Father, I want to do as you wish."

"I don't believe you." He glanced at his wife.

"Father, I have only one wish. Please grant me this. I'm going to get married."

Yong Ju stared at his son, dumbstruck. He looked over at his wife and saw that she was looking downcast.

"What are you talking about now? Why do you want to get married? Please explain."

"I love someone now. She is… she is… Mr Choo's daughter."

Yong Ju stiffened. He squinted at his son. Suddenly, he slapped his son right across the face. He rolled up his sleeves and went briskly to the cabin in the middle of the courtyard to get his shovel. He headed back towards Hyun Suk. His wife ran to him, trying to restrain him. At the same time, she called out to the neighbour, like before, but he wasn't there.

Yeon Mee's House.

Yeon Mee's slender face was now swollen. She didn't look like herself any more. Her mother was sitting against the wall of the room, crying. Yeon Mee was crying too. Her father was sitting, panting and gasping, on a chair nearby. He said to his daughter,

"You are a stupid girl. You have left a mark of disgrace on our family. If you have something to tell me, say it now. It's your last chance."

"I love him."

Once again, Mr Choo became enraged. His face grew redder and redder.

Hyun Suk's House.

Hyun Suk was expecting his father to strike him with the shovel and shout at him like an earth-shattering meteor. However, suddenly Yong Ju fell silent, as quiet and meek as a gentle woman. He threw the shovel aside and sank down on to the stone table. His head drooped on to his chest. Hyun Suk had never seen his father calm down like that. He felt nervous. What was going on in his head? Was this the moment to tell his father about Yeon Mee's pregnancy before he heard the news? But then, it was too late because his father was already walking out the gate, looking back sadly at his wife and son.

The next morning.

Yong Ju was standing out in a field. Tall pampas grass was waving in the breeze. He broke off a strand of the grass, sat down on the ground, and began tracing an image in the dust with it like a small child at play. He then put the grass between his teeth and lay back looking up at the sky. He pondered the last ten years of his relationship with his son. He had thought that he had always had the upper hand with Hyun Suk, and he was beginning to understand at last that he had been rather selfish. Now, the realisation was dawning on him that it was time for his son to find his own path in life. He really did feel a deep love for his son, but it had been buried for so long. He knew that it was time to adjust his attitude and try a different approach on him.

Yong Ju walked back through the pasture, past the field of pampas grass. He heard someone calling him from afar. It was Hyun Suk's Haegeum teacher, running after him, panting and out of breath.

Yong Ju asked him, "What's up?"

"You have to go to the police station right now. Mr Choo and Constable Huh have just arrested Hyun Suk and they've already left," he gasped.

Yong Ju and Hyo Jun arrived at the police station. Yong Ju entered the room and yelled, "Where is Constable Huh?"

All the policemen looked at him. In the corner, the senior constable stood up slowly from his chair. Yong Ju approached and confronted him, raising his voice,

"Why did you arrest my son? Where is he?"

Constable Huh was anxious, knowing Yong Ju's reputation for aggressive behaviour. He tried to calm him down by offering him a seat. Yong Ju shoved the chair in anger and frustration, and shouted, "Where is my son?"

"Don't shout at me! Is this your house? You always speak too loudly whenever you come in here!" said the constable, loudly in return.

Yong Ju quietened down and looked around the room.

Constable Huh said, "Mr Choo has made allegations against Hyun Suk."

"And just why has Mr Choo made allegations against Hyun Suk?" demanded Yong Ju.

The constable didn't know what to say and looked around the room at the other policemen, who were watching him closely. Yong Ju also noticed them, and they looked at him with hostility, so he spoke more softly, "What is the problem with my son?" he said, politely this time.

Constable Huh couldn't tell Yong Ju the real reason behind the arrest. The truth was that his father and Yong Ju's father were friends, and he and Yong Ju had gone to the same high school. Another policeman, who understood the constable's dilemma, said loudly to Yong Ju, "Hyun Suk has been arrested because he is being accused of committing an act of sexual violence against Mr Choo's daughter!"

Hyo Jun was standing at the door. His eyes met Yong Ju's. Yong Ju took a gulp of air, and Mr Huh again offered him a seat.

"If I sit down there, it doesn't change my circumstances one bit. Just tell me, what act of sexual violence has my son committed against Mr Choo's daughter?"

"Please sit down," said Mr Huh.

"No! Just tell me now! Tell me exactly what he has done!"

Mr Huh said, "Oh shit!" under his breath.

"Did I hear you say 'shit' to me? To me, your senior? You should not say 'shit' to me!"

Yong Ju was creating a scene, so Mr Huh reverted to his official role as a policeman.

"Do you know that Mr Choo's daughter is pregnant? She is having Hyun Suk's baby, and it was conceived through sexual violence. That is rape. That is why Mr Choo has made the allegations. Do you want to know more?"

Yong Ju's eyes met Hyo Jun's again. Yong Ju was shocked into silence. Hyo Jun was also shocked. Usually, Yong Ju felt powerful. But now, he was defeated and humiliated. He couldn't believe the situation he was in. He needed to hear the truth from Hyun Suk himself. Yong Ju walked quickly to the police cell. He knew where it was. He had been in there himself several times. Two policemen blocked his way. He pushed them aside roughly, seeing his son in there alone behind the bars. Their eyes met. They remained silent for a few moments. Yong Ju then asked his son,

"Is it true, what they say?"

Hyun Suk did not answer.

A woman wearing a hat appeared at the door. She came inside. All the policemen stopped to watch her. She looked around. Her eyes landed on Yong Ju in the corner. She walked towards him. It was Yeon Mee. She bowed to Yong Ju. Then, she saw Hyun Suk. Hyun Suk saw her coming in and was surprised. Yong Ju was also surprised. Even though she tightly wore a hat, her bruises and swollen eyes were apparent. Those watching her were shocked at the sight of her.

Yeon Mee turned to the policemen and spoke assertively,

"The reason I came here is because something's wrong. I did not tell my father I was raped. It wasn't like that at all!"

When she had finished speaking, Yong Ju's face burned with anger. He pushed over the chair and kicked the desk in rage, shouting, "The police have believed Mr Choo's one-sided statement, and there is absolutely no evidence for putting my son in jail!"

At that moment, Mr Choo walked frantically into the room through the main door. Yong Ju caught sight of him as he was kicking the chair, preparing to throw it, and turned his attention on him. Several policemen ran to restrain him.

Mr Choo quickly walked over to his daughter, and said, "Why did you come here? Come with me now." His voice was urgent with stress and anger.

Yeon Mee didn't move.

Her father took her by the arm and dragged her, as she wouldn't walk on her own. He put his arms around her to try to coax her out.

Yong Ju shouted sarcastically, "You tried to turn my son into some kind of criminal. But your daughter has made it quite clear that she has a different view of what happened."

Mr Choo stopped and turned around.

Yong Ju continued, "Do you think your social status is that powerful just because of your money? And you think you can bully my innocent son with it? If your power were to have any influence you would have gained it by unfair means with your money – just like the piano school. Can you deny that?"

Mr Choo let go of his daughter, crossed his arms, and walked towards Yong Ju menacingly, and hissed at him, "I could spit on you now, just as you did to me before, but I won't do that because it is primitive. I know nothing of my daughter's statement. It means nothing in any case, making such a statement in an insignificant police station such as this. My daughter would have never opened her mind to a low life like your son. He raped my daughter."

At that, Mr Choo went over to Yeon Mee and grabbed her hand again pulling her towards the doorway. Yong Ju was enraged by Mr Choo's insults, and rushed at him, fists ready, but the police restrained him.

The Next Day.

Yong Ju visited the police station again. Constable Huh told him that Yeon Mee's statement was not important at this time because it was Mr Choo who had laid the complaint against Hyun Suk. The case was therefore required to go before a prosecutor. The accused had been transferred to the central police station and was being detained there.

Yong Ju left the station, pale and worried. He went straight to the town councillor and appealed to him to intervene in his son's case against the injustice Mr Choo had inflicted on him in such a high-handed way. However, the town councillor already knew about the case, and had decided to take the side of Mr Choo and the mayor. He was not willing to help Yong Ju. He only repeatedly told Yong Ju to hire a lawyer. Yong Ju left the town councillor's house in a state of torment at the injustice he felt. He was extremely worried that his son would be imprisoned for a long-time while awaiting trial. He felt a consuming hatred for the mayor, Mr Choo, and the town councillor, which was growing all the more now.

The Day After.

It was nearly noon. Yong Ju had slept in because he had had too much to drink the night before. He heard the Haegeum teacher's loud voice outside announcing that Yeon Mee's statement had been overturned and Mr Choo's statement that Hyun Suk had committed rape had been accepted.

After hearing the news, Yong Ju had visited many people in the Haegeum-making industry. He appealed to all of them for support in this matter. However, most of them had been influenced by the opinion of the mayor. Yong Ju started to realise that he had failed to remain on good terms with people at times like this, which he had needed to do when confronting authority. Previously, when he had been working for the establishment of a Haegeum School, people had been on his side, always praising him for his efforts. Now, they had completely turned against him and would not support him. Whenever he left their homes, his heart sank deeper and deeper into a void. Depression was overwhelming him. He realised that he was powerless to do anything to help his son. He felt broken, fragile, and isolated. He was losing all connection with the world around him. He finally realised how crucial it was to keep good relationships with others. After this, he fell deeper into alcoholism. He pondered about how he could overcome this hardship. Finally, he came up with the idea to create a counter-charge against Mr Choo and the mayor. He thought that would be his best option.

#

Late one night, Yong Ju left the bar. He had drunk too much as usual. He headed off home. From his store room, he brought out two large plastic containers. Liquid was sloshing around in them and although his legs were giving way under their weight, he managed to hoist the containers on to his bicycle as well as some other items.

Yong Ju arrived at the building that was being turned into a Piano School. The wooden framing was almost complete. He crept up the pathway, pouring oil onto each of the pillars that were holding up the structure. It was a grand building, about the size of a quarter of a soccer field. He climbed up the radio mast which was located next to the piano building. He then hopped into the piano building from the radio mast and poured oil everywhere. He climbed down to get the other container, climbed back up, and went all around the edge of the building, pouring out more oil. He went back down and stood, looking at the Piano School from in front. He smoked a cigarette with his trembling hand and took a deep breath. He took some oily paper from his back trouser pocket, scrunched it up into a long taper, and lit it. He took it across to the edge of the building and carefully set each pillar alight. Soon, a fire was raging. The wind was blowing in just the right direction…

By the next morning, the news of the destruction of the Piano School by arson spread around quicker than the speed of the descending morning mist.

A crowd gathered in front of the destroyed building. It was obvious who the arsonist was. There, in front of the building, hung a large white banner which read,

'There is a conspiracy against my son, Hyun Suk. He is a victim.'

Yong Ju came out of the hospital walking between his wife and son, Hyun Meen, who were holding on to him. His arms were wrapped in bandages from the burns. His clothes and face were smoke-blackened. They walked slowly down the steps where a police vehicle was waiting. Two policemen got out, handcuffed Yong Ju, and shoved him into the police car like a piece of baggage. Hyun Suk's mother was still in a state of shock from the awful news about her son and Yeon Mee and the frightful accusation against him. And now, here was her husband being driven away in handcuffs in a police car. After they disappeared, despair overcame her, her legs folded, and she collapsed on to the pavement. It wasn't only Hyun Suk's mother who were devastated by all that had happened. Even Mr Choo himself was beginning to feel the burden. The night before the fire, he hadn't been able to sleep, worrying about the truth of the situation between his daughter and Hyun Suk. He was mindful of the moral questions of right or wrong. His mind was confused and tormented. He contemplated what he should do to put things right. However, the news of the arson left him no choice. He erased the conflict in his head. He felt his heart swelling with indignation and came to the conclusion that he has done the right thing in making an accusation against Hyun Suk. He ended up thinking that he would let this father and son rot in jail.

#

Mr Choo waited at his gate for a visitor.

After a short while, Constable Huh came towards him on his bike. He got off his bike and walked over to Mr Choo. Mr Choo handed him his formal complaint about the arson.

112

"Another son of a bitch for you, another crime. Father and son can go to jail together," Mr Choo declared.

Mr Huh took the papers and put them in his official bag. He said, "I have big news for you."

"What news?"

"Hyun Suk has confessed everything."

"What! Everything?" Mr Choo's mouth had fallen open.

"He pleaded guilty to the act of sexual violence against Yeon Mee. He has admitted everything."

Mr Choo was surprised as he had begun to wonder if Hyun Suk really had done it after all.

Mr Huh went on, "It's good for our case that he has confessed so soon. The investigation must have gone very well. The next investigation will also go quickly, I'm sure."

Their eyes met, but Mr Choo looked uncomfortable. He tried to hide his thoughts, looking away from the constable.

"Well, Constable, is that all? Did he give a detailed statement? When, how, where? Or did he just state that he was guilty?"

"Yes, of course. He gave a detailed statement. It happened at Ill Ryong Mountain beside *So Yang Lake*, in his secret piano practice den. My superior has asked me to go to the mountain and search for evidence. I will be heading out there tomorrow morning."

Mr Choo looked more uncomfortable because he was worried that they would uncover evidence that denied his credibility.

"You don't have to worry," said Mr Huh, "This investigation is complete. I just want to search for evidence to satisfy my deliberations. Your daughter has been asked to come to the Central Police Station tomorrow to make a statement. We will ask her, regular, standard questions but just in case, could you please talk to her to make sure she doesn't make a statement like her earlier one? I have to go now."

Mr Choo asked Constable Huh, "Do you know exactly where the practice den is?"

The same night at Hyun Suk's den.

Mr Choo brought a lamp and shined it on the wall. A miniature Harley Davidson appeared. He moved the lamp around the room and saw stereos, record players, and a lot of books about jazz. On another wall, he caught sight of a traditional woman's coat on a hanger. He went over and had a closer look. He thought it must be his daughter's coat. Angrily, he put the lamp on the desk and began to tear at the garment. He threw it to the floor so he could do a proper job of ripping it to shreds. He clenched his teeth, screwing up the torn fragments and throwing them away. In rage, he kicked the hall desk, breaking its leg. The desk collapsed. He grasped the broken leg and turned around, looking for anything that might belong to his daughter. He put the lamp on the floor to shine more light in the room. When he saw a light switch, he turned it on. He caught sight of the piano for the first time. He stood still, staring at it. He walked over to it and saw some yellow papers on it. It was a music score. He picked it up and read it. The title was Jazz Lovers Part One: Ballad plus Bossa Nova. In the corner of the score, it said, 'Dedicated to my love, Yeon Mee.' He looked more closely at it, reading it page by page, holding it under the light. After a while, the look on his face slowly changed. He became serious, absorbed, and peaceful. He approached the piano. Standing there, he began to play it slowly with one hand, holding the score in the other. He turned around in search for a chair. He found one, brought it over to the piano. He sat down, turned the pages of the whole score of Jazz Lovers Part One, and played it right through.

When he had finished playing, he sat still, motionless. He was mesmerised. He knew that this was a fine composition, very professional. He was drawn to play Part One again even though he had already finished. Insects were buzzing around him, making it difficult to concentrate. He got up, chased out the bugs, and began to play some portions of Part One. He loved it.

He looked for more parts of the score. There had to be more. The power of the music had enthralled him so deeply. His mood of fury had dissipated entirely. Now, he was like an archaeologist searching for relics. He craved to find more of that score. He needed more detail; anything would do, even if incomplete. At last, he found it: Jazz Lovers Part Two: Rock plus Fusion Jazz and then later he found Jazz Lovers Part Three: Classic plus Jazz. He scanned closely through them all, concentrating intently on each page. Shifting on his seat, he played Part Two, completely involved in the music. The second part was a combination of romantic, sad, happy, and passionate moods - a total cross-over of style. He really wanted to play Part Three, but suddenly became conscious that maybe he shouldn't. It was as if, if he did, he would be stealing every last secret of Hyun's Suk's heart. A deep respect for the young man crept into his mind. Despite his conscience, he was still tested by the temptation of playing the last part. But ultimately, he closed the piano, thinking that it wasn't the right thing to do.

Finally, Mr Choo left the secret house. He stood outside, holding his lamp, and gazed at it. It was hard to leave.

The next day, early in the morning.

Mr Choo went to the central police station. After he left the police station, Hyun Suk was free to go home later that day. The reason was very simple. Mr Choo had dropped every complaint against Hyun Suk.

18
The Present

"It would be a miracle if he recovered." the doctor had said to Yeon Mee two days before. When she heard these words, she felt distressed and desperate. She remembered how she had fallen in love with Hyun Suk long ago. There had been no doubt about it. Until now, she had thought that the passing of years had lessened those feelings of love.

'So why are you still here beside him? Is it because of your son? Do you still love him after all this time? Is that true?' Yeon Mee was asking these questions to the woman staring back at her in the mirror of the hospital bathroom.

Hyun Suk opened his eyes. Yeon Mee was glad to see that he was awake now, as he had been shouting out all sorts of things in his sleep.

"You're awake now?"

Hyun Suk looked around the room, forgetting where he was at first. He looked at Yeon Mee, then asked, "Is the operation over?"

"The operation was two days ago. You haven't completely woken up yet."

He tried to pull himself up in his bed but found he was too weak. His face was pale and jaundiced. He felt nauseous from all the medication.

"You fell asleep yesterday afternoon. You've slept a solid

twenty hours. That's good."

He was surprised to hear this. Twenty hours, he thought to himself. Does this mean she has been here since yesterday?

"My family, where are they?"

"Your granddaughter had to go to school, and your son starts his special Haegeum Cultural Assets Scholarship programme tomorrow. He had to leave last night."

Hyun Suk had thought about the way Yeon Mee was speaking. The way she was talking about his son and granddaughter's whereabouts. It was new and refreshing. Then she said to him,

"Now, you must eat something and rest. Look after yourself."

'Now, I have to eat good food and rest?' Suddenly feeling sad, he thought that she would say her goodbyes, and leave him again. He looked away from her so that she wouldn't see his face.

"If the operation had been delayed any longer, you might have been driven crazy," she said in an effort to comfort him.

Hyun Suk then opened his mouth, "Yeon Mee, can I ask you something?"

She raised her eyebrows.

"When I leave the hospital, how about you play with me?" he suggested. Pondering further, he added,

"For such a long time I've wanted to play Jazz Lovers with you to your father because we never had the opportunity long ago. I hardly expected at that time that we would be parted forever."

Yeon Mee remained silent a few moments, then said, "It isn't forever, now that we've met up again like this."

They looked at one another, their eyes locked.

19
The Past

Standing near a small bush, Hyun Suk, wearing a suit, put a large bag down beside him. He looked around as if waiting for someone. But no one came. After half an hour, he picked up his bag and hid it amongst the branches of the bush.

He drew nearer to Yeon Mee's house and looked around to survey the situation. Something felt wrong. It was dark, yet there were no lights. The house looked unoccupied. He approached the front gate slowly. It was cross barred, locked and fenced. Perplexed, Hyun Suk turned and walked briskly away.

Hyun Suk then went to the Piano School. Light was shining from the window. He looked inside to see if he could find Mr Choo or Yeon Mee. Many students were practising the piano but neither Mr Choo nor Yeon Mee were there. There was an assistant piano teacher in Mr Choo's place. Then, he heard a woman's voice, "Hello, Hyun Suk?"

He turned around quickly. A female student stood there. She was Yeon Mee's friend.

"I thought you would come here. Are you looking for Yeon Mee?"

Hyun Suk quickly nodded.

She continued, "I was surprised when Mr Choo's whole family left town today."

Hyun Suk stared blankly at her.

"They have left for good. Their house was sold a couple of days ago."

"Who told you that?"

"The town councillor. He came here this afternoon."

The town councillor's house.

The town councillor looked tired and dejected. He said, "When I heard Mr Choo was leaving town, I was astounded. He sold his house under the market price, right after the fire."

"Sir, did you find out where they were going?"

The town councillor shook his head, "We just greeted each other, but I never heard where they were heading. I presumed Mr Choo's daughter would have at least told you. That's unfortunate."

Hyun Suk was crushed and, with his heart sinking, asked, "Did Mr Choo's daughter leave with her family?"

"Do you really think Yeon Mee would be staying here alone without her family? That couldn't happen. She didn't want to go with them, but her father got very angry and slapped her across the face. It seemed like she didn't know Mr Choo planned to leave and was suddenly forced to leave with him."

Hyun Suk was deeply shocked. He gasped for air, feeling as if the ground was rising up to swallow him. He had always thought this love story was going to be very challenging, but he had believed true love for her could overcome all difficulties. He had read many stories where love conquered all barriers. He enjoyed those kinds of inspiring stories. He had grown to love Yeon Mee so much but now, she was gone. His mouth was dry, and he felt so overwhelmed that he couldn't focus on anything anymore.

He returned to Yeon Mee's house in hopes that she might just have left some kind of message for him, but he found nothing.

#

Late at night, the town councillor came quickly to the courtyard of Hyun Suk's house, calling as he came,

"Hyun Suk! Hyun Meen! Hyun Suk's Mum!"

Hyun Suk was sleeping on the deck, surrounded by empty bottles. The town councillor went up to him and shook him, trying to wake him up. Hyun Suk had drunk so much that he couldn't even open his eyes. Hyun Meen came out of his room. The town councillor said, "Hello Hyun Meen. The police have just called to inform me that your father is in emergency care right now. When he was being taken into jail, he lost consciousness." At that moment, Hyun Meen's mother came out of her room in her dressing gown, wondering what all the commotion was about.

Nobody was present when Yong Ju died. He had already passed away by the time his family arrived at the hospital.

The policeman asked the doctor for the cause of death. The doctor replied that he had had a cardiac arrest which stopped the blood supply to his organs, causing a cerebral infarction. At that moment, they noticed the family's presence. The doctor came over to Hyun Suk's mother and informed her that her husband had passed away. She slumped to the floor. Yong Ju's two sons bowed their heads.

20
The Present

"Here's a change of clothes for you," said Yeon Mee, putting clothes and boots on the table of his hospital room. There was a white T-shirt, a black leather jacket, blue jeans, a pair of socks, and black boots. Yeon Mee was wearing the same style of clothing and a bandana in her hair. She removed the drip from his arm and urged him to get up and get dressed.

Hyun Suk looked at her in surprise, "What's happened? What are you doing?"

"We are going out now. I'll leave the room for a moment, and you get changed."

Hyun Suk stood up, gazed at the clothes, and decided to put them on.

After a while, Yeon Mee knocked at the door.

"Come in!"

She opened the door carefully. Hyun Suk felt shy. She opened the door wide and came in, exclaiming happily,

"You look fantastic!"

She liked how he looked, dressed like that. She was smiling like a teenager. She picked up her handbag and took out some hair gel. She squeezed some out on to her hands, rubbed them together, and put it on Hyun Suk's hair. At that moment, the nurse came in. She looked at them both, then went back outside to check on the room number. She noted that the drip was out, and that the patient had changed his clothes. What's happening here? she thought to herself. Ignoring the nurse, Yeon Mee spoke,

"Okay, are we ready? You look really nice. Let's go." Hyun Suk didn't move, so she pushed him gently out of the room, taking no notice of the nurse.

"Where are you going?" asked the nurse.

"Don't worry about him." Yeon Mee said, "I'm going to take good care of him, and we'll be back before dark."

The nurse just stared; her brown eyes wide open like big brown grapes. Yeon Mee and Hyun Suk left the room. They walked along the corridor to the lift. Doctors and nurses watched them leave in their unique attire. They got in the lift. Hyun Suk's supervising doctor came towards them with a startled look on his face to say something. Yeon Mee just put her finger to her lips and smiled at the doctor. The lift door closed.

They left the hospital and walked along by the wall. Yeon Mee told Hyun Suk to close his eyes. She took his hand for about ten paces, went around a corner, and stopped.

"Okay, you can open your eyes now!" she said. His eyes remained closed.

Again, she said, "Come on!" still, he didn't open his eyes. He just stood there, holding her hand as if he didn't want to let go. Finally, he opened them. There in front of him was a Harley Davidson.

"Remember thirty years ago, how you told me that the sound of the Harley Davidson was the best sound in the world, and that whenever you heard it, every bone in your body came alive, just like with jazz?"

Hyun Suk looked into her eyes. Yeon Mee smiled at him.

She went up to the Harley Davidson. There were two helmets. She handed him one and took out some dark glasses from her handbag for him to wear.

"We'll have a date today, enjoying the Harley Davidson!"

Hyun Suk looked at Yeon Mee, mystified. He shook his head, saying he had never driven one.

"Don't worry! I'm going to drive it!" she said, hopping on the Harley, "You get on the back and hold on tight."

They rode all through *Choon Chun* province. Many people watched them as they passed, surprised to see a woman driving a Harley with a man holding on tightly to her back.

They parked outside some ice-cream shops and fast-food stores. They were like two teenagers out on a date. They drove along *Choon Chun* Boulevard, which was lined with beautiful yellow gingko trees. There was a lake beside it...

Soon they arrived at the jazz café. It was built like a sailing boat on two levels. Parking in front, they went inside the café. People stared at them in their Harley Davidson-style clothing, and especially at Hyun Suk, an aging man with long hair. At the front was a stage where a group was playing jazz music. Yeon Mee looked around for somewhere to sit. A waiter came towards them smiling and directed them to a corner table. Once they were seated, a man playing the guitar waved 'Hello!' to Yeon Mee, having just finished playing a jazz piece. A woman came out from behind the stage, carrying a Haegeum.

"We're just in time," said Yeon Mee to Hyun Suk. She was watching the woman on the stage, "let's listen. I've heard her before. She's a good Haegeum player."

Yeon Mee was so engrossed in watching the woman tune

her Haegeum that when the waiter came to their table, she ignored him and just said abruptly, "I'll order later."

Hyun Suk was not accustomed to seeing Yeon Mee behaving rather rudely like that. Usually she was a sensitive, kind, and gentle woman. He said to the waiter, gently,

"We will order in a moment, thank you."

The woman started to play. About eight bars passed, it wasn't traditional Korean music but a jazz repertoire. Hyun Suk and Yeon Mee's eyes met. Listening to jazz being played on the Haegeum made very deep feelings rise from within his soul. Shortly, the other members of the band began to join in, and it was marvellous to hear. Hyun Suk's eyes were shining. Yeon Mee shifted her attention from the stage to Hyun Suk, watching him come alive with the music. The Haegeum player was reaching a point of ecstasy in her music. Hyun Suk looked intoxicated as if he was high on drugs. To Yeon Mee, it was as if he had been transformed since leaving the hospital. He was swaying in time to the music. She loved watching him. Her shoulders swayed to the music too, as the Haegeum player reached a thrilling finale. Everyone applauded. Hyun Suk and Yeon Mee look at each other steadily for a long time. She whispered in his ear, "That woman plays here quite often. A couple of weeks ago I asked her how she came to play jazz on the Haegeum. She said she had always played traditional Korean music in the past, but she had discovered that jazz gave her such a great feeling that she decided to switch over permanently."

Hyun Suk smiled at the thoughts and memories that arose in him on hearing this. His smile was from thirty years ago. Yeon Mee hadn't seen that prolonged smile since finding him again in the hospital. She wanted to stand up and tell the world that she had made him smile. A big, perfect smile today! She imagined waving her arms in the air and crying, 'Waahhhooo!'

The waiter came back over to take their order. After they ordered, a guitar player came over, excused himself to Hyun Suk, and whispered something in Yeon Mee's ear. Reluctantly, she said, "I am not dressed right and I'm not ready to play just now."

The man looked very disappointed. He said, "But the boss is here, and he's requested that particular song. He says he'll raise our pay next month, so we have to please him. As you know, it can't be played without the piano." Petulantly, she asked,

"Why didn't the usual pianist come today?"

Hyun Suk nodded at her, indicating the stage, encouraging her, "Go on. You play." She got up hesitantly and said, "Okay, I'll play. But just this one song."

She got up on to the stage and sat down at the piano fingering the keys, getting a feel for them. The other players watched her, and she gave them a signal after three beats. After sixteen bars the melody began. It was one of Hyun Suk's favourites on the Haegeum: *I Will Wait for You.*

Thirty-two years ago, Yeon Mee and Hyun Suk had played his arrangement of that piece together for the first time in his secret den. This song had brought them together.

A few weeks before, Hyun Suk had told Yeon Mee in the hospital, that whenever he heard that song, it made him think of her. It always made him feel both happy and sad. Now he began to understand why this piece was being played at this place and time. After listening a little more, he knew exactly what was going on. The version they were playing was Hyun Suk's own arrangement, a fusion of Korean traditional music and jazz!

Yeon Mee was looking at him, smiling. All the players were also watching him. He blushed and felt deeply moved. Yeon Mee had planned this day just for him. The Haegeum player came over to him and handed him the Haegeum, smiling. He covered his face with his hand and smiled in uncertainty, not knowing what to do. Many guests around the tables were watching him. He shook his head, which could mean 'yes' or 'no'. It became a 'yes'. He took the Haegeum from her and stood up. The audience applauded as he walked up onto the stage.

He sat in front of the microphone, turned to look at each player, nodding hello to them. They kept up the rhythm until Hyun Suk was ready to start playing. As he began playing, many people stopped what they were doing to watch him. The way he played, and his body posture appeared to be rather strange but unique. His body bent forward as if he was a hunchback, but that was just his playing style. Yeon Mee was well aware of the way he played, awkward yet soulful. She watched him carefully, keeping him company in her heart like she used to back in the days. The audience began to follow his rhythm and sway as he built up speed. As he increased the pitch of the groove, the rhythm also increased in speed. Some people stood up and cheered. Gradually, everyone started showing their admiration of his playing. Even the two chefs came out of the kitchen to have a look at what was going on and the waiters stood in awe, watching.

Hyun Suk finished playing. Everyone was standing now, applauding wildly, shouting for an encore. Yeon Mee got up from the piano and walked over to Hyun Suk, whispering something in his ear. He looked at her with surprise because he didn't know that she and the band knew about Jazz Lovers Part Two. Since he never had a chance to bid farewell to her long ago, he had given the score to someone else to give to her, but he never knew if it had actually reached her. After Yeon Mee and Hyun Suk reunited, Hyun Suk suggested that they play Jazz Lovers together. Hoping that she would agree, he also expected her to say that received the score many years ago. But she hadn't mention anything about the score. He wanted to ask her if she had received it, but in case she hadn't, he didn't want to fluster her. As always, he would never want to put her on the spot regardless of how curious he was.

All these years, he would never have imagined that today, he would be playing Jazz Lovers Part Two with her. He felt overwhelmed. Tears came to his eyes. He held his breath and looked over at the band members, nodding that he was ready now. Yeon Mee saw that he was ready, went over to the lead guitar player and spoke to him, then went back to the piano and sat down. The clapping faded while the band leader was tuning his instrument. He then signalled to the band and the encore began. It was Jazz Lovers Part Two, Rock plus Fusion Jazz…

Perhaps it was the rock that was infused into the song in Part Two, the crowd soon became infatuated with excitement. Alongside the other band members, Yeon Mee and Hyun Suk's backs started dripping with sweat. Yeon Mee even rose from her seat and zealously played the piano on her feet. Hyun Suk's tied hair became loose in the midst of his head banging. His hair cloaked his entire face, but he was solely focused on his playing, with his head still rocking around in the beat of the music…

After the encore performance, the audience's clapping

and cheering seemed to never cease. They had no choice but to play another piece. The leader of the band was rattled in awe, he didn't expect such a response from the audience. He looked over at Yeon Mee and Hyun Suk. Yeon Mee thought it would be best to calm down the overly excited crowd because Hyun Suk's condition couldn't keep up with this energy. The band selected a ballad, as Yeon Mee suggested, as their final encore song. *I Will Wait for You*, Jazz Ballad Version.

As the song was playing, Hyun Suk felt the perfection of their performance and realised that the band members, including Yeon Mee, had been practicing this song countless times. A song that he had also arranged himself...

Yeon Mee and Hyun Suk arrived back at the hospital. Hyun Suk changed out of the Harley clothes that Yeon Mee had brought and folded them carefully. He looked around for the bag. It was hung on the handle of the window. He put them in the bag. Yeon Mee gently knocked at the door, "Are you finished?" she asked.

"Yes, come in," he replied.

Hyun Suk noticed that she had also changed out of her Harley Davidson clothes. For him, today had been a dream— music, passion, happiness, riding, and playing together. Words could hardly convey the intensity of the feelings he had experienced today. Now, it seemed as if only silence, sadness, and darkness remained between the two of them. Hyun Suk brought the bag of Harley Davidson clothes over to Yeon Mee.

"They are yours. Keep them," she said.

She looked up at the clock on the wall and said with a somber tone, "I have to go now."

Hyun Suk also noticed the clock, then said, "Thank you

for today. I've never played the Haegeum as well as I played it today."

"And I've never played the piano as well as I played it today."

In the silence that followed, they didn't look at one another, looking away instead. To break the long silence Hyun Suk asked,

"Since when did you learn to ride a Harley?"

"When I lived in Japan, Harleys used to always pass by my house. When I heard them, I always thought of one man. The first time I heard a Harley engine it was very loud. But after a while, the noise became something like a beautiful instrument. Just as it had been for that man. My uncle had one and I learned from him. I now have one in Japan."

Hyun Suk was impressed. She said, "Can I ask you something?"

He raised his eyebrows.

"You told me when we met again, that you had never forgotten me, not even for one day."

Uncertain of what she meant all of a sudden he looked blankly at her.

"How did you never forget about me, not even for a single day? It's a bit silly, isn't it, for thirty-two years?"

Hyun Suk wasn't expecting that question expressed so directly and so strongly. He blushed. He turned to look out the window.

"You don't want to answer me?" she asked.

Still no answer.

"How did you live only thinking about one woman all your life?"

He didn't speak.

"How did you live alone for thirty years without even holding another woman's hand?"

Still no answer.

"Do you really expect me to believe that?" she continued, but still, he did not answer her.

Even though the questions were serious, her eyes were playful, dancing a little.

Hyun Suk raised his voice and said, "You're asking me silly questions. I have never been able to forget jazz, which is only music. So, how could I have forgotten the only woman I have ever loved?"

For a moment, there was silence between the two. She was touched by his sincere response. She felt grateful for what he said and wanted to say something to express how much she appreciated him, but there was not enough time now. Sung Jae would be waiting out there in the carpark, looking at his watch, and wondering why she was taking so long. She looked up at the clock again but found that she shouldn't stay.

"I really must go now," she said.

Yeon Mee walked slowly towards the door, and stood there, holding the door, looking back at Hyun Suk.

Hyun Suk said to her, "Concentrate on your father now, don't think about me anymore. You have done so much for me since we met again, it's time to look after your father. I'll look after myself now."

"Before you leave hospital," she said, "we should be able to meet up a few more times."

Hyun Suk didn't expect this answer. He was really pleased.

"I'm going now," said Yeon Mee.

She left the room.

After she had gone, he picked up the bag of Harley Davidson clothes, went over to the wardrobe and carefully put them away. He went to the window and looked out, desperately longing to see her once more. Suddenly, he remembered something that he had forgotten under the bed, some red roses. He had never given her flowers before.

He hurried out of the room towards the lift, but it was too far away. He turned back and took the staircase.

He went out to the lobby looking for Yeon Mee. He saw her going out the main entrance and hurried, trying to catch up with her. A car pulled up. Sung Jae got out and went around to the passenger door to open it for Yeon Mee. Hyun Suk hid himself behind a pillar. He kept the roses behind his back. It was a luxury car. The driver was wearing a tie and looked well-groomed and wealthy. He was good-looking and smart, his hair firmly gelled back. Hyun Suk recognised him, the famous jazz pianist and university professor, Sung Jae Yoo.

Hyun Suk watched the car until it disappeared. He thought about Sung Jae's music and how he played the piano on his TV music shows. He turned away and sat down on a bench with the roses beside him. The sun was going down behind the mountains. Darkness fell, but Hyun Suk continued to sit there on the bench…

Yeon Mee was in the passenger seat beside Sung Jae. She remained silent on the way home from leaving the hospital. Sung Jae glanced at her, sensing her mood. He was waiting for a chance to ask her something.

"I had a call from my mother yesterday and she gave me a date," he said, cautiously.

Yeon Mee said nothing.

"Why won't you answer me?" he asked.

"Sung Jae, I need a little more time."

He was offended. He carried on driving then, all of a sudden jerked the steering wheel and pulled over to the side of the road. He hit the steering wheel, took a deep breath, pulled out a cigarette from his briefcase, held it downwards, twirled it and looked out at the horizon. Yeon Mee saw in his eyes that he was very sad. Some time ago, she had told Sung Jae that she had a son with Hyun Suk. Sung Jae felt more depressed now than he felt then. His sadness was like a great looming shadow between them. She imagined his mind must have been burning into white, dusty coals. She couldn't rid that image from her mind. Sung Jae put the cigarette back in his briefcase and turned the ignition on again. He wanted to show his resentment and ask her honestly how she could expect him to wait any longer. However, he couldn't take it out on her because he loved her so much.

"We've arrived. You're home," Sung Jae said abruptly. They had driven in silence ever since stopping at the side of the road. Yeon Mee just sat there.

"We're here. You can get out now," he said, becoming angry.

"Do I have to get out of your car now when we haven't even spoken to each other?" she asked, also feeling anger. Sung Jae had mixed feelings about the irritation in her tone. He thought she shouldn't be feeling angry. They looked at one another without speaking. However, he saw in her eyes that she was sorry. He had conflicted feelings about her apology. On one hand, she still loved him. On the other, she might also still be in love with Hyun Suk. If that was true, it was like some

133

kind of love triangle which left him feeling jealous. He tried to erase the second possibility from his mind. He wanted to believe in Yeon Mee. They have been committed to each other for a long time. Love always holds risks and challenges. This is one such moment. He was trying to stand back from the situation, so as not to be so self-centred or blind. It was time he stopped trying to weigh up these things. It was much better just to trust her and to believe that all was well between them. Love could not be forced. He knew that this was the best way. So now, his eyes were saying 'sorry' to her. Yet, he blurted out his frustration. He couldn't control his words, as he could do with his mind.

"We're here now, you need to go home and take some time to rest," Sung Jae said. Yeon Mee got out of the car very slowly.

Sung Jae drove off.

Yeon Mee sat still in her home, looking at the white wall directly in front of her. She was deep in thought with her handbag still over her shoulder.

Hyun Suk was wearing a suit and tie, his hair slicked back, and he had shaved. Maybe he wanted to look as well-groomed as Sung Jae. He looked in the mirror, holding the roses.

"Hi, Grandad!"

Hyun Suk turned around, and there was his son, daughter-in-law, and granddaughter at the door. Jeong Soo and his wife looked quizzically at him, wondering what had happened to him as he was not dressed in hospital clothes but was wearing a suit instead. Hyun Suk suddenly felt shy and embarrassed. He ruffled his hair and loosened his tie to take it off.

Yeon Mee washed her face, came out of the bathroom, and stood at the desk in front of the bookshelf, looking for one large book in particular. She found it, flicked through the pages, got the yellow booklets, and looked at them. It was a music score. There were three booklets, 'Jazz Lovers Part One, Part Two and Part Three. She moved over to the piano, sat down, and began to play.

Sung Jae's car pulled up outside Yeon Mee's house. He had decided to come back. He got out and went towards her gate. He stopped when he heard the music and listened to it for the whole time she was playing before pressing the button on the gate.

"Who is it?"

"It's me."

There was no answer. He waited at the gate. It took a while until she opened it. During the short time she had before opening the door, she had put on make-up and had tied her loose hair back into a neat bun.

The two looked at each other in silence until Sung Jae broke it. "I'm sorry about before. I couldn't control my feelings and wasn't very nice to you, so I decided to come back. My mind was unsettled. We need to talk."

"Come in."

They sat across from each other in the lounge near the piano. They didn't speak for some time. After a while, Sung Jae asked gently,

"How long do I have to wait for you?"

She hesitated.

He said, "I think a promise is very important between lovers. It measures something very deep. You promised me up

135

until after his operation, didn't you?"

She didn't speak.

"Okay, I'm not too concerned about that broken promise, and I understand why you are being so kind to him. I also understand you had a son with him. But what next? Did you ever consider about my work commitments and my parents' happiness?"

Yeon Mee couldn't look him in the face any more and looked down.

Sung Jae covered his face with his hands and sighed.

"Our promise was to our family, so if we break it, it will also be broken with our family, not just us. In every relationship of this world, a promise made between lovers is also a promise made to each of their families."

When she still said nothing, he continued,

"I'm sorry I'm talking so frankly. My mother was angry when you postponed the date to meet my family for the third time and she asked me if our love was one-sided."

Yeon Mee looked directly at Sung Jae, then looked down again.

Sung Jae stood up and paced the floor, waiting for her to break her silence. Still, she didn't say a word. He felt a tightness in his chest. He knew he must not lose his temper but rather retain his self-control. He looked at her as she looked down at the floor. He guessed that she was feeling low. Suddenly, he let go of his urge to push her. He slowed his breathing down to make himself feel peaceful. Yeon Mee, still looking down, said, "Sung Jae, sometimes we can't explain the reasons behind things we do in life. I have never changed my feelings towards you, even now, and I do understand how you feel."

"Are we still going to be married?" Sung Jae asked.

"Yes, I have never lost my love for you, but I just don't know what to do right now. Sung Jae, have you ever felt hopelessly in love in your life? Real, true love, only to have it shattered? Has that ever happened to you?"

He did not understand what she wanted him to say.

"Whenever I thought of him, I always hoped that he was happy. But all these years he has been becoming even more miserable. I wanted to do something for him thirty years ago, but I never got the chance, so I need to meet those obligations now. If his doctor hadn't told me that his chance of survival is extremely low, those obligations would have remained as mere thoughts."

Yeon Mee tried to calm herself down with deep breaths. Without interrupting, he looked at her. She went on, "So that's why I'm asking you now for more time. If my love for you wasn't deep, I wouldn't have told you about my son or my former lover and all the history of my relationship with Hyun Suk. If I wasn't deeply in love with you, I wouldn't have been so openly sincere and honest with you, Sung Jae."

Yeon Mee's eyes became red, and tears welled up in them.

"Could you please wait for me a little longer?" she asked quietly.

Sung Jae looked away, breathing heavily through his nose without replying. He paced the floor again, then caught sight of the score of Jazz Lovers on the piano. The words 'Dedicated to my love, Yeon Mee' were written on it. He looked over at Yeon Mee, to see if she had noticed. She was looking down at the floor in her current state of torment. He began to read it more closely. Soon he asked,

"Can I play this?"

Watching him, she paused, then nodded in reply.

He sat down at the piano and played with his right hand, slowly, then both hands together, from the beginning. It was as if the score belonged to him, so fine and natural was his playing. He was a brilliant pianist.

When he had finished playing Jazz Lovers Part One, the look on his face showed that he was moved by the beauty of the music as it was so sad and deep. Then he turned to Part Two, glanced through it and looked across at Yeon Mee's face for permission. Understanding his unspoken question, she nodded. He breathed deeply, preparing himself. After a pause, he began to play, and went straight into Part Three as well. While playing, he was concentrating and giving it his all. After playing, he searched for the name of the composer but couldn't find it. On the last page of Part Three there was the date when this score had been composed. It was thirty-two years ago! He couldn't believe how this beautiful avantgarde music was composed thirty-two years ago. Its composition and form were entirely contemporary as well. Sung Jae was curious. Who had written this piece? He examined the score again. There was no composer's name. For a split second, Hyun Suk's name had come to his mind, but he erased the thought immediately as Hyun Suk was a traditional Korean music player. He forgot that he had been arguing with Yeon Mee. He asked her who wrote it, exclaiming,

"It's amazing! How could it have been written thirty years ago?"

Yeon Mee looked down, saying nothing in reply.

21
The Past

One fine sunny day.

Hyun Suk's family were making Haegeums in the courtyard. Their father was no longer there so Hyun Meen had taken over his role. The exterior of Hyun Suk's house had been renovated. The old brown roof tiles had become blue. The storehouse and kitchen had new blocks and timber work. The gate was re-painted. The fence was new, and there was hedging along it. Hyun Suk now had long hair, a long beard, and his skin was dark from the sun. His face was melancholic. It spoke of his emptiness and loneliness. When he had been with Yeon Mee, he had looked happy, passionate, and full of energy, but now he looked as if somebody had cut off his shadow and had left him bereft. A small candle for Yeon Mee was alight in his heart but it could easily be extinguished at any moment. A week ago, he had received a letter, sender unknown. The stamp was Japanese. The sight of it had brought Hyun Suk's spirit alive with hope. It was a simple letter with only seven lines, but the last three spoke of an unexpected blessing:

My daughter, Yeon Mee, is carrying your child. This will be detrimental to her future. She will give birth to the baby in Japan, and then we will hand the child over to you...

Hyun Suk had worried that Yeon Mee's father might force

her to terminate the pregnancy. If that happened, everything between them would be completely over. But for now, it wasn't. He would be able to keep hold of his dream. He wondered who would bring the baby to him.

22

Hyun Suk had just finished his final attempt at the examination for traditional Korean music on the Haegeum. When he completed his performance, the head examiner, seated in the middle, smiled at him with satisfaction and said, "Thank you for your excellent performance. But while you were playing, I felt rather uncomfortable and anxious. Do you know why?"

Hyun Suk looked at him.

"This was your final opportunity. I was hoping that you would continue playing our traditional Korean music and not do what you did last year."

Hyun Suk said nothing.

"Can I ask you a favour?"

The other two assistant judges watched the head examiner with interest. This was unusual.

"I have never made a request before to a student, but I would like to make one now. Could you please play one more song for me especially? I would like it to be in a western-style."

Everyone stared at him in astonishment. Hyun Suk didn't take his eyes off him. The assistant judges looked shocked. The head examiner smiled at them as if saying, 'off the record'. He looked over at Hyun Suk again and said, "What do you think? Can you play another song for me?"

Hyun Suk hesitated. The head examiner said,

"It would be nice if it was jazz."

While Hyun Suk continued to hesitate, still surprised, and watching the faces of the other judges, the head examiner assured him, "Don't worry, you have already completed your examination. I'm now asking you to play a song that has nothing to do with the examination."

Hyun Suk slowly began to play Jazz Lovers Part One Ballad Version...

Outside the door, the Haegeum teacher, who had been calmly listening, jumped up in amazement when he heard the western-style music. Why this? Annoyed, he went over to the window to see what was happening and listened anxiously.

While Hyun Suk played, he closed his eyes and began to remember how it felt to be given his baby son...

A Couple of Days Before.

Hyun Suk was standing alone. Behind him were the mountains in the setting sun. The day was coming to an end. In front of him lay a long road. He stood a few metres away from the road, waiting. Eventually, a black car came towards him. It slowed and stopped a distance away from him. Out of the car stepped Yeon Mee's mother, carrying the baby in her arms. For a while, Hyun Suk and Yeon Mee's mother stood staring at each other in silence. They slowly approached each other. Without a single thought of the baby in his mind, Hyun Suk looked inside the car to see if Yeon Mee was there. Her mother shook her head slowly. Only the driver was there. Hyun Suk looked away at the sunset in disappointment. Yeon Mee's mother then handed him the small baby, a bundle of personal belongings, the baby's immigration documents, and passport. Then, she gave him a ring and said, 'This is from my

daughter.' As she was getting back into car, Hyun Suk asked
her to wait a moment. He went over to her, taking an envelope
from his pocket. In it, was the score of Jazz Lovers Parts One,
Two and Three, bound in the yellow booklet. Her mother took
the score and got back into the black car which did a U-turn
and disappeared into the distance... Hyun Suk stood in the
field, with the baby in his arms. The sun had gone down. The
wind was blowing.

Hyun Suk played the final part of the melody loudly. When
the music ended, the Haegeum teacher saw that the head
examiner was giving him the thumbs-up. Then, he understood.
The head examiner clapped for a long time. He said,

"Last year, when you played that jazz song, it was very
dynamic and cheerful, but today you played it with such
melancholy but also very beautifully. I didn't know that our
Haegeum could cover such a wide range of emotions. Thank
you for that. Once again, I feel that the Haegeum is the greatest
instrument and the way you played it is proof of that."

Hyun Suk had never heard such praise from a figure of
authority before. He wanted to smile and thank the head
examiner, but he couldn't because the other two judges may
not appreciate this kind of music. So, Hyun Suk remained
calm, saying nothing. The head examiner spoke to him again,

"Mr Hyun Suk, you could become a great cultural asset if
you continue with our traditional Haegeum playing. We don't
want young players changing over to Western music. What do
you think?"

Hyun Suk answered,

"Each and every instrument is made solely to play music,
no matter what the genre is. I just want to play music,

regardless of whether it is classical, jazz or traditional, and just to play music itself without classifying it. If I am going to be a cultural asset playing the Haegeum, I will simply be playing music and spreading the love of music and of the instrument. My love of the music will bring life and love of music to all people."

When Hyun Suk finished speaking, all the judges sat in solemn silence.

23
The Present

Two people were seated on the pleasant outdoor patio of a café, looking out over a wide lake and alpine mountains. They were Hyun Suk and Yeon Mee.

"I can't remember the date," he told her, "maybe fifteen years ago, when early one morning it was raining, then around noon the clouds lifted, and it became a clear sunny day. An hour or two later, it clouded over again, and by mid-afternoon the wind got up and it began to thunder. Lightening flashed, hail pelted down, and it began to sleet and snow. Soon, the wind dropped again, and large snowflakes began to fall. Then, step by step, the horizon cleared, and the sun returned just as twin rainbows formed arcs across the sky. Never in my life have I experienced such a day, with the weather changing so dramatically in such a strange and beautiful way. Today, it feels like that I am experiencing such a precious day once again. It is because of you, Yeon Mee Choo."

He said so much and felt shy. He was overcome with sadness; his voice had dropped to a murmur. Strong east winds from across the lake couldn't swallow Hyun Suk's declaration from echoing in Yeon Mee's ears. Before he spoke, she was calm and peaceful. But now, a sense of profound melancholy and nostalgia came over her. She was incapable of returning such beautiful words. It was very painful to her because she knew what the outcome was going to be. Today was a turning point. She knew she could not respond as he would have wished. The two of them were silent looking out at the lake. Hyun Suk began to speak,

"I have one question for you. Why did you want to have Jeong Soo when you could have had an abortion?"

Before this question, Yeon Mee thought she could end their love-story forever. But now, somehow, this question unnerved her. She couldn't reply to Hyun Suk's challenging question. She no longer knew what to do. But she couldn't avoid this question. There was a long silence. She finally spoke,

"I wanted to have your baby. When my father demanded that I have abortion, I threatened to move out. My parents were afraid that I would run away and go to you so, we made a deal that I would stay home and give birth. When my baby was a few days old, he disappeared. My parents took him to you. I have never seen the baby's face since he was born. The hospital told me that the baby had to be put in an incubator due to a complication. But that was a lie. My father and the hospital colluded with each other."

Suddenly, she stopped talking. She felt overwhelmed by emotion. She turned to look away. Hyun Suk quietly waited for her to speak again. After a while, she turned back to him. But she couldn't continue her words and just gazed at him. Hyun Suk was looking down at the ring on his finger.

"This is the ring that your mother brought to me when she came with Jeong Soo. This ring was my hope but I'm starting to think you might not have given it to me."

Yeon Mee looked away again. Tears began to fall. She tried to say something, but it wasn't easy,

"You are right. That ring wasn't sent from me. My mother was lying to you. That ring was her idea alone. When I asked my parents where my son was, they showed me the photo of him that they had taken before they gave him to you, and the ring was there. I felt terribly sad for you and still do now. I am so sorry."

Yeon Mee wiped the tears from her eyes. She continued, "Even though it was the ring my mother gave you... I went on hoping. I thought that ring would be a symbol of hope for our future. I had a dream of going back to Korea. But I couldn't because after my son disappeared, I became very sick. Nobody knew the name of that illness. For three years, I couldn't do anything. I couldn't even walk or talk, but a Japanese doctor helped me. For three years, he devoted himself to my recovery. He saved my life. We started living together... And yet, every day I still thought of you and my son. I should have at least sent you letters... but I couldn't. I realised living with him, that I was just a woman absorbed in a man's life..."

She continued after a while, "I thought that someday, you might come looking for me. I hated myself for expecting you to come looking for me when I didn't do the same for you."

Hyun Suk avoided looking at Yeon Mee. Then looking back at her, he said,

"I missed you so much. I did go looking for you. For two years I searched. Finally, I got your address in Japan. That was twenty years ago."

Yeon Mee was amazed. He continued,

"I saw you with your husband and daughter. I couldn't speak to you. Your family looked so beautiful."

"Did you really come to Japan? Did you really see me?"
Hyun Suk nodded.

147

Yeon Mee wanted to say something but couldn't. Finally, she asked, "Why? Why then? When you saw me with my beautiful family, Hyun Suk, why didn't you find another woman?"

Hyun Suk put his head down then lifted it. He looked into her eyes directly, saying,

"It must have been my destiny to only love one woman."

His short but profound reply made her feel sorry and guilty. She felt like she was about to sink deep into the ground and back into the dark times. His words were going around and around in her head. She didn't know where to go, or what to do. She wanted to run away from all this sadness. After a moment of silence, she spoke, "I'd like to take you to meet someone tomorrow. Will you come?"

His eyes questioned her.

"I'll pick you up at the hospital around three. Is that okay for you?"

Slowly, he nodded.

"I'd like you to bring your Haegeum with you."

He wondered who he was going to meet but didn't ask. Yeon Mee picked up her handbag and stood up. Hyun Suk got up too, ready to leave the café. At that moment, the music at the café changed to another piece, Kenny Dorham's *Blue Bossa*.

Thirty-two years ago, in her father's piano class, Yeon Mee had played this song. After that class, Hyun Suk had followed her home and simply told her that her playing had been very beautiful. He had then turned around and left. That was all he said, but she knew it was a declaration of his love. The impact of those words was more heartfelt than the simple words, 'I love you' could have been.

They both looked at one another and sat down again. They didn't speak. They looked out over the lake to the mountains where the sun was piercing through. The sky was streaked with purple and orange, and the ripples on the lake glittered. They sensed intense feelings of sadness and beauty. A seed of love had sprouted long ago in them from *Blue Bossa*. Hearing it once again conjured all their memories and feelings of love for each other.

The next day.

Yeon Mee drove over a winding dirt road. The roads were very slippery from the rain. She asked Hyun Suk,

"Aren't you wondering where we're going?"

"I am."

"Then why haven't you asked me?"

"Of course, I'm wondering, but I'm just happy that I am with you, so it doesn't matter where we're going or what we're going to do." Yeon Mee smiled.

She continued driving until they came to a wide clearing framed with trees and greenery. She parked beside a very beautiful flower garden. Behind it was a large traditional Korean home with a decorative garden made up of trees and rocks; the composition looked like a traditional folding screen.

They got out of the car. A woman came out of the house, waved and smiled at Yeon Mee. She was the housekeeper.

Hyun Suk was wondering where they were. He indicated the Haegeum with his eyes, and Yeon Mee nodded to bring it inside.

The housekeeper came over to Yeon Mee, saying, "Hello, Madam. How are you?"

"I'm doing well, how about you?"

"I'm fine."

"How's my father doing?"

"He's very well. He's waiting for you inside. Please come in."

Finally, Hyun Suk realized that Yeon Mee had taken him to her father's house. As he stood there in shock, unsure what to do, she asked him, smiling, "Do you know where we are?"

Hyun Suk just nodded. She understood his hesitation and discomfort. She didn't want him to be sad. She just wanted a cheerful atmosphere. Hyun Suk retrieved his Haegeum from the car and followed her into the house.

The housekeeper opened two sliding doors. On the far wall were a lot of book shelves and a white piano. The same one Mr Choo had had long ago at the piano school when he was Hyun Suk's teacher. On the right was a door into another small room. They went and stood near that door, both now feeling nervous.

"It's me, father, Yeon Mee," she announced, opening the sliding door and going in.

Mr Choo was seated on the floor in front of his desk. Behind him were mural panels of Korean art. He was peering over his reading glasses towards the door. He looked at the man standing beside his daughter and wondered who he was. Hyun Suk also almost didn't recognise the man by the desk. Hyun Suk saw that the old man looked very gaunt and frail. He had dark spots of pigmentation on his face, arms and legs. However, he still sat with a straight back. He had a head full of hair and his sideburns remained as they had before, as if time had had no effect on them. Yeon Mee put her handbag down and went over to her father, taking his hand and saying,

"How are you, father?"

Mr Choo welcomed his daughter in reply, holding her hand tighter in his, trying to say something. Words didn't come out. She understood what he was trying to say and replied, "Yes, I am eating well, no problem. Look, I've even gained some weight around my waist!" Her father smiled.

He looked over at Hyun Suk. Yeon Mee also looked at him, then she said, "It's Hyun Suk."

The two men looked at each other. Hyun Suk put his Haegeum down and bowed down on his knees before Mr Choo in a gesture of deep respect. Mr Choo also bowed from the waist, but he was looking uncomfortable because he didn't yet know who he was bowing to. It was a difficult situation for Yeon Mee too, having to explain to her father who the man beside her was.

"Father, do you remember Mr Yang Yong Ju? This is his son, Mr Yang Hyun Suk."

Mr Choo couldn't remember Mr Yong Ju. He blinked, watching his daughter and this man with her. Yeon Mee went over and took out the Haegeum from its bag and carried it over to her father. Mr Choo was still confused. She went over to her handbag and took out a yellow binder and put it down in front of her father. It was the original score of Jazz Lovers. Mr Choo looked at it and read it, then his eyes opened wide with surprise. He looked from his daughter to Hyun Suk, amazed. Yeon Mee read his thoughts and said,

"It was just by chance that we met again."

Suddenly a cloud of sadness came over the old man's face. Hyun Suk felt ill at ease, thinking that Mr Choo wasn't pleased to see him. Mr Choo got up and struggled to walk over to him. Yeon Mee tried to help her father, but he didn't want any help. He took a long time. It took a lot of effort to get close to Hyun Suk by himself. He looked into Hyun Suk's eyes. Suddenly he grasped his hand firmly, wanting to shake it. Hyun Suk was at a loss and didn't know how to respond to this. He looked around the room anxiously and caught Yeon Mee's eye. Mr Choo was trying to say something to him, but his voice just came out in a croak. Yeon Mee told him what her father was trying to say.

"He's asking about his grandson."

Hyun Suk was amazed. In the past, Mr Choo had treated him coldly, but now his attitude seemed to have changed. He asked himself if Mr Choo really was asking about his grandson, Jeong Soo. Hyun Suk felt mixed emotions, but he had to provide an answer before anything else.

"Your grandson is very well. Thank you."

At this, Mr Choo grasped Hyun Suk's hand even more firmly. Hyun Suk could see how sad his eyes were. Hyun Suk thought perhaps he was trying to say he was sorry for his behaviour in the past. Overwhelmed with a variety of emotions, Hyun Suk felt waves of sadness, happiness, relief, regret, and disappointment breaking over him. Yeon Mee had picked up the score of Jazz Lovers from her father's desk. She said to Hyun Suk, "A long time ago, in the secret piano place in the mountains, you told me that you wanted to play this score to my father."

There was great emotion in Hyun Suk's eyes as he looked at her. In an even softer tone, she asked him, "Do you remember? You told me that you would like to tell my father that this score would show greater love than simply telling my father you loved me. Do you remember saying that? So, here is your chance. Today is the day."

Even though she was speaking lightly, Yeon Mee was

feeling very sad. It was as if teardrops were pouring from her heart.

Again, she said to him, "After my mother left the baby with you, she returned to Japan. For a whole year she tried to decide whether or not to give the score to me. She contemplated not giving it to me at all and just throwing it away. Finally, however, she handed it over at the end of the next year. Without it, the following thirty-one years would have been much harder to bear. One day, I played it to my father. I played the Jazz Lovers Ballad Version, and when I had finished, my father remarked that the song must have been written by someone who was crazy in love. I thought it was the first time my father had ever heard it. 'Who wrote it?' he asked me, even though he already knew. I couldn't answer him. After many years, my Japanese husband died. One day, my father asked me to play all the versions of Jazz Lovers for him. After I had finished playing, he told me in confidence that he already knew who had written the score and that he knew about the secret place in the mountains."

Hyun Suk's face registered great surprise. She said, "After I played Jazz Lovers for my father the first time, his comment about the song writer being madly in love was always on my mind. Hyun Suk, do you understand what I mean? My father recognised our love, all that time ago, after he had played Jazz Lovers."

A long silence filled the room…

Yeon Mee finally broke it, saying, "Hyun Suk, I would like to play it with you. Can we do that?"

Hyun Suk looked at Mr Choo.

Yeon Mee asked her father if they could play the score now, and he nodded.

She walked with Hyun Suk into the room where there was a piano. Hyun Suk brought his Haegeum with him and Yeon Mee showed him his seat. He sat down, and began to tune the instrument. Yeon Mee sat down at the piano and spread out the score.

Then, they began to play Jazz Lovers Ballad Version Part One, continued by Part Two and Three…

While they were playing, Mr Choo listened carefully, watching them intently. He tried to stand up, and with difficulty, moved over to his desk, searching for something. He found his pen, some notepaper, sat back down again, and started to write.

"With true love, everything seems possible, but there is one pitfall. True love cannot control its own destiny. It was not your destiny to be with my daughter. But even now, I can see that your love for her has always been true through all the storms of life. That love is even more enduring than the love which gets what it wants. Yours is not a love that fades but one that stands the test of time. Hyun Suk, I am really sorry. Please try not to be too sad."

Hyun Suk and Yeon Mee finished playing. Mr Choo expressed his applause through his smile. He was holding the note he had just written and handed it to Hyun Suk. Curious of its contents, Hyun Suk took it and bowed in respect before Mr Choo. He went over to the corner of the room to have a look at what was written there, turning his back on Yeon Mee and her father so that they wouldn't see his feelings. She wondered what was in the letter but assumed it was a private matter between her father and Hyun Suk. When she saw the empty look on Hyun Suk's face, her eyes showed him that she understood and shared his sadness.

Yeon Mee and Hyun Suk left her father's house. When they first arrived, it had been raining, but now it was much heavier. There were thunder and lightning and wild gusts of wind. Hyun Suk noticed none of this, still preoccupied with the letter that filled his mind. He realised now that Mr Choo had acknowledged the history of their love, both the good times and the bad. Just like that, in a split second, Hyun Suk felt a tiny spark of hope rising in him.

The downhill road was slippery and wet. Yeon Mee's car wheels were skidding. The wipers were on full speed.

"Be careful!" Hyun Suk exclaimed. Yeon Mee slowed down. A pond appeared on the left. There was a lot of mud and the road was steep. The car began to skid. Yeon Mee braked, and the car spun sideways. She accelerated, trying to change direction, but the wheels had locked. The car stalled. Hyun Suk tried to open his door, but it was stuck fast. The side of the car was buried in mud. Yeon Mee also tried to open her door but couldn't.

"Neither door is working, what shall we do?" she cried.

Hyun Suk wound the window down to have a look, "I'm going to try to get out the back door," he said.

At first that door wouldn't open either, but after pushing it harder he managed to free it. Yeon Mee told him to grab an umbrella from the boot. Hyun Suk opened the boot and found the umbrella, but it was no use to him. He was soaking wet already. He looked at the car stuck in the mud and saw that there was little they could do.

"We have a problem here," Hyun Suk said, "we need help." He went over to a small hill and walked up, trying to see if there was a village nearby. He could see nothing.

"How far is the nearest place?" he asked her.

"There is nowhere near here." She replied, "The nearest town's too far away."

"We need a tow," he said.

Yeon Mee opened her handbag and found her mobile phone. She tried calling but there was no signal. She shook her head, looking at him. Hyun Suk went over to a hill on the other side of the road to see if there was anything there. He saw some lights way in the distance. He went back to the car and told Yeon Mee,

"I saw some lights. We are going to have to walk. We need help, it's going to get dark soon. Do you have another umbrella?"

Yeon Mee shook her head.

He looked in the boot again. There was a large sheet of plastic. He asked her if he could use it. She nodded. He climbed into the back seat with the plastic. He took out the Haegeum and string from the case and unwound some string. He had scissors in his case. He cut a length of it and carefully wrapped the Haegeum in its case in the sheet of plastic and tied it firmly with the string. He couldn't leave his Haegeum in the car. Yeon Mee could have the umbrella, and he would carry the instrument in its case on his back, safely wrapped to keep it dry.

They set out walking towards the lights. There was mud all over their clothes. In spite of the umbrella, Yeon Mee was getting very wet. As they got closer to the lights, they renewed their efforts, speeding up. They stopped in front of a neon sign, the 'Smile Motel'. Underneath the sign was another one in neon lights which read 'Water beds available, 24hour Adult Movies, Deluxe massage service. Privacy guaranteed, No cameras.'

Yeon Mee and Hyun Suk glanced at each other awkwardly.

Yeon Mee said, "We have no choice, we have to get out of this rain."

They went into the motel. They entered the lobby and walked towards the reception desk. Yeon Mee was shivering. She went up to reception.

"Excuse me. Is there anyone here who could help us? We've broken down, stuck in heavy mud, some way from here, and we can't move our car."

"That's too bad," said the receptionist. "Where is your car exactly?"

"It's on Duma Mountain Road."

"Is it on the open road or the dirt road?"

"It's on the dirt road."

"I'm really sorry, but in these bad weather conditions and at this hour, we won't be able to get a tow-truck."

Yeon Mee and Hyun Suk looked at each other. Her lips were blue with cold. Cautiously, she said to Hyun Suk,

"I have to warm up, what do you think?"

The receptionist asked her,

"Do you want a room?"

"Yes, we need two rooms."

"I'm sorry, but we have only one room left."

Hyun Suk and Yeon Mee felt uncomfortable. They stood for a while looking at each other, trying to decide what to do. Then the receptionist looked outside and saw a car approaching the motel and said, "You need to make up your mind. It looks like another guest will arrive any minute."

Both of them looked away then back to the receptionist.

"We'll take the room, thank you," said Yeon Mee.

Hyun Suk sat alone in the motel lobby near the café while Yeon Mee went up to the room to take a shower.

The bell rang at reception.

"Front desk here. Yes, he is… Sure," said the receptionist, putting the phone down.

He went over to Hyun Suk and said, "Excuse me sir, your partner is waiting for you now. She wants you to go up to the room."

The door was slightly ajar. "Can I come in?" asked Hyun Suk, hesitating at the door of the room.

Yeon Mee called to him, "Come in." He peered through the gap and scanned the room. Steam was coming from the bathroom. He cautiously entered the room. Yeon Mee was already sitting on the end of the bed, wearing the same wet clothes, using a handkerchief to rub the mud from her trouser legs.

"I'll wait outside. You can take a shower now," she said.

"Are you okay? Do you feel warmer now?" Hyun Suk asked.

Yeon Mee nodded. Hyun Suk put his Haegeum down. Walking towards the bathroom, he heard a phone ring. It was Yeon Mee's. She went over to her handbag, considering if she should answer or not. She looked over at Hyun Suk for a second, still hesitating. Hyun Suk looked back at her briefly, noticing that she felt uncomfortable and worried. He went into the bathroom quickly and closed the door. Yeon Mee answered the phone.

"Hi. Yes, it's me… How are you? What? Where?" she went over to the window, looked out, and saw that rain was still pouring down. Sung Jae was standing there, without an umbrella, holding his phone to his ear. Yeon Mee felt overcome with embarrassment and concern.

"I'm coming down now." She said to him. Desperately, she tried to think what she should do now. Then she went over to the bathroom door and knocked gently.

"Hyun Suk, I'm going outside for a little bit," she said in an anxious voice.

Hyun Suk opened the bathroom door. He hadn't yet undressed.

"What's happened?" he asked.

Yeon Mee looked down then up at him. She didn't respond.

"I see." He nodded. Slowly, she went over to the door. He said,

"You'd better take your handbag. Early tomorrow morning, I'll go and try to move your car to a safer place. Leave me your key."

She thought, he understands my situation so well. He knows I'm committed to someone else.

Yeon Mee reflected on the choice she had made and thought of all the moments she had experienced since meeting up with Hyun Suk again. This one was by far the hardest. She looked across at her handbag. At first, she left it there and began to walk towards the door. Then, she turned back again painfully, picked up her handbag but put it down again, pondering again what to do. Decisively, she picked it up and left the room.

After Yeon Mee had left, Hyun Suk came out of the

bathroom. He looked to where the handbag was and found it was no longer there. Crushed with sadness, he leaned back against the bathroom door and gazed slowly around the empty room. While she was still there with him, he felt strong and confident. But these emotions were an ephemeral spark like that of a shooting star. However, he sought to gather his emotions to keep calm and decisive, accepting the situation. He took a deep breath, but nothing could placate his feeling of total dejection and abandonment. He felt shocked, devastated, and physically distressed. Maybe the symptoms of the virus of jealousy were seeping into his whole body, cutting his heart into pieces.

Yeon Mee went through the lobby and out the main door. Sung Jae was still standing out in the heavy rain, soaking wet. She went out into the rain and stood there, looking at him as if to say, 'I'm sorry, Sung Jae.'

They stood in the rain for a while. Sung Jae came close to Yeon Mee, looking into her eyes. Without saying a word, he went into the lobby with her following behind. When he saw the café, he went inside and chose a table in the far corner. They sat down and gazed into the distance. After about five minutes, Sung Jae at last spoke. His voice was stern.

"Can you please explain what's going on?"

She didn't speak, looking down.

"Why did he have to meet with your father?"

She didn't respond.

"You don't want to answer me?"

When she said nothing he went on, "Okay. Even though your car got stuck in the mud and it was getting dark, how did you manage to come to this obscene motel in particular and get a room with that man? How can you explain that?"

She was still silent.

"Do you expect me to understand all this?"

When she would not speak, her face flushed red, he tried to calm down a little. Coldly, he said,

"Okay, our engagement is off. It's finished." His voice was firm.

Yeon Mee looked at him at a loss. It was unexpected.

In the meantime, Hyun Suk had come out of the room and hidden behind a partition in the café, he overheard their conversation. He heard Sung Jae say, "Even though you betrayed me today, I still don't hate you. I remember you have said that love itself is not enough to love someone. Now, I understand that. We are not destined to be together in love. I don't regret our times together, but one thing disappoints me - you haven't kept your high moral standards. It was wrong of me to follow you today, but it was only because I love you so much. I have to go now. I'm sorry, it's over."

He got up to leave. Yeon Mee stared at him, knowing that there was nothing she could do to stop him. She didn't even try to persuade him to stay. He was leaving, and she just watched him leave. At the same time, Hyun Suk watched Sung Jae walk outside. He watched Yeon Mee. After he had gone, Yeon Mee sat motionless at the café table, staring out the window. Her face was drained of colour, her expression was very sad, yet she also had a look of confidence. Why did she look like that? Because she had no regrets about what had happened. She had always been honest with Sung Jae. She had always loved him, and still did even now. It seemed she was always apologising, and yet, she felt she had been right in each and every decision she had made.

Yeon Mee stood up and left the café. She had a look of

self-assurance, as if she was not afraid any more. She went and stood in front of the motel gates and saw that Sung Jae's car was gone. She stood there, lost in thought for a while, and then headed back into the cafe. Sitting there she pondered what to do next. She stayed there for a long time before getting up and going towards the lift.

She knocked at the door of the room. There was no answer. She knocked again, "Hello Hyun Suk? Hello, are you there?" Still, he didn't answer. Slowly, she began to open the door, then opened it wider. Then, she stood rooted to the spot, gasping, her hand flew to her mouth. She began to scream. Shaking violently, her legs collapsed under her and she sank to the floor.

"No, oh no!" she cried out in the depths of grief and despair...

Hyun Suk had cut the curtains and his Haegeum's strings and made a noose, suspending it from the light fixture. His body was hanging there, limp and still.

"Help!" she called in despair, "Somebody, please, come and help me!"

#

"I saw him at the hospital for the first time in thirty years," she sobbed in despair. "I haven't had time to ask him all the things I needed to know... and now it's too late, too late... our love was so sad, and yet it was so beautiful... through all those years I wanted to see him again, and to see the son I had never met. And then I saw my son for the first time, there in the hospital... how could I have walked past Hyun Suk and my son and not said anything, how could I? Who can understand my situation? You asked why I brought him to my father. How can I ever possibly hope to explain how important this was? For the last 30 years, he kept a photo of me, but right before he passed away, he defaced it with water. Do you know what that means? For thirty years he has lived thinking only of me. Thirty-two years, Sung Jae! I have always spoken with total sincerity... I have been completely honest with you, hiding nothing. But now, I know there is something even more important than passionate love, and that is to never, ever forget the one that... you have loved..."

Sung Jae sat listening to Yeon Mee's heart-felt words. Still sobbing, she choked back tears. He saw that she was traumatised. She was suffering deep shock and loss. She was inconsolable. He held her hand, helping her to sit down. He sat down next to her by the door of the motel room. Several policemen and a doctor had arrived to investigate the scene of death. The investigation, which included a statement from Yeon Mee, took a while. Hyun Suk's body was still hanging there.

A policeman came over to Yeon Mee and said,

"You need to come to the police station to add to your statement further as we need more information. I am sorry to ask this. I couldn't ask before. You were too upset. Who are you in relation to him?" she said nothing. She looked at the policeman and then back at Sung Jae, hesitating. Finally, she said, "He's my lover."

24

His ashes were scattered into the lake from the hill near his secret piano place. It was the same place where he had once tried to take his own life. His son, Jeong Soo, had wanted to bury his father's body, but he changed his mind after receiving a call from Yeon Mee. She told him that his father would always miss that place, and she believed his ashes should be scattered there. Jeong Soo didn't contradict her suggestion and followed her idea completely.

But Jeong Soo thought, why didn't she attend at least one of the days of his funeral period? So, why not? Today was the last day of his funeral, yet she didn't come. From time to time, he looked around for her, but she was not there.

The sun was sinking into darkness. The guests had all left. Only Jeong Soo and his family remained there. Jeong Soo watched the sun setting behind the hills and the currents in the river moving and fading beneath his gaze. His wife and daughter stood a short distance away, watching him with sadness. Clouds gathered and a mist was rising all around them. As they turned to leave, Jeong Soo heard the sound of someone coming up the mountain path. He had a feeling that it was Yeon Mee. He was right, it was her. Yeon Mee had her reasons for being late. She looked carefully around to see if there was anyone else there apart from Jeong Soo and his family. Even at that distance, her eyes met Jeong Soo's. Yeon

Mee raised her skirt a little so she could walk faster. She came up the hill and paused in front of them. Both Jeong Soo and his wife bowed their heads in recognition. Yeon Mee responded with a small smile. She stood there, gazing at the sunset, the mountain, the river, and the trees that were all around her. The place where she stood was exactly where the secret den used to be. She moved over to their little daughter and patted her head kindly, smiling without speaking. The little girl smiled back at her. Everyone remained silent for some time. Yeon Mee needed to take control of the feelings that were overwhelming her. She felt she must conceal them. But Jeong Soo was looking at her piercingly with a questioning look. He wouldn't stop looking at her. Noticing his stare, she wanted to escape as soon as she could. She wanted to offer her condolences, but she was feeling quite overcome herself. She saw how very sad they were, lost and lonely in their misery. Yeon Mee's eyes became red as she tried to control the tears. She turned away so they wouldn't see her grief. Looking back at them once more, briefly, Yeon Mee turned and disappeared. She couldn't stay any longer just in case her feelings of deep sadness exploded out into the open, exposing her.

Jeong Soo couldn't believe that she would leave without speaking, without saying anything at all, leaving no message. He thought this could be the last time he would ever see her. He had so many questions to ask, so many words to hear from her. But she left without even saying goodbye.

Sung Jae sat in his car at the bottom of the hill. He watched her coming, saw her face, but couldn't decide whether or not to start the car. She got in and shut the door. He tried to think what the best thing to do was. He looked carefully at her, then turned on the ignition. As tears began to pour down her face, he passed her a handkerchief. She wiped her eyes. Sung Jae turned off the ignition and got out of the car. He thought Yeon Mee needed to be alone.

"I'm all right, Sung Jae. Don't worry, you don't have to get out, thank you," then she said, "I really appreciate you coming to the funeral with me, Sung Jae."

Sung Jae drove her home and stopped outside the gate. He said, "Please take some rest. I haven't had a chance yet to speak to you about my concert this coming Sunday. I don't know if you want to come, you may not feel up to it, but I would really like you to. Do you think you can make it?"

Yeon Mee didn't answer.

25

It was late autumn, and the crispness of early winter was in the air. The first snow was falling today. Yeon Mee saw the whiteness all around her as she came into her front yard. Fallen leaves were scattering in the wind, brushed with snow. The leaves on the garden side were mostly covered with snow. She stopped walking and looked at the leaves that were covered in snow for some time, thinking how life itself is like the lifecycle of the fallen leaf - it can be tossed about, torn, and withered before finally being destroyed. She guessed that those snow blankets were providing security and purpose for their existence. Yeon Mee thought, 'Even though the leaves love to be nourished by the water from the snow, when the noon sun arrives, the snow will melt away and the leaves will once again be exposed to the drying conditions of the sun'... Yeon Mee suddenly thought that all the leaves must feel bewildered, and this made her feel sad. Although she hoped that the sun would be mindful of the leaves condition and would protect them, she knew that nature must go on and nothing would change. Yeon Mee bent down to the pond, picked up all the leaves that were sitting in the snow, and let them fall into the pond. She thought they would be better off in the water and would live longer, hydrated. Perhaps they could even live until this Christmas? Her car was parked at the side of the front yard. She hopped in, closed the driver's door and looked at the leaves on the pond and smiled.

She drove down the beautiful street towards the university. Red maple trees lined the street, and a blanket of snow covered the bushes beneath them. In the grounds of the university, she could see bright yellow gingko trees. They were so lovely. She turned right towards the Arts Department and parked behind the grand arched theatre building where Sung Jae was preparing for a concert. Yeon Mee wondered why there were hardly any cars parked there. A few students were riding their skateboards, their breath steaming in the cold weather. It was strange that no people were going into the theatre. She looked inside the lobby then checked her watch, hesitating to go inside. She took her phone out of her handbag and was about to make a call when a young woman appeared at the hall doors and came over to her, bowing respectfully.

"Are you here for the concert?"

"Yes," replied Yeon Mee.

"My professor has asked me to guide you to your seat. Follow me, please."

Yeon Mee followed the student into the theatre. There was nobody there; only one guest: herself.

The student led her up a staircase saying, "I'll show you to your seat."

Yeon Mee's seat was right in the centre.

"Here's your seat. The concert will begin soon." the student smiled secretively.

Yeon Mee felt quite strange.

A few moments later, the lights dimmed. The stage curtain started to rise bit by bit, coming to a juddering halt. For a while, there was silence. Then, a spotlight came from the side, highlighting the piano at the centre of the stage. There were footsteps and there he was: Sung Jae. He bowed to his one audience. At once, Yeon Mee understood what was happening. All the events of the recent past raced before her eyes and she felt very emotional. She let out a deep sigh. Sung Jae sat at the piano and immediately began to play. He looked at ease. He was playing the song as if he had practised for some time and had written it himself. She knew what he was doing. Just as she expected it was 'Jazz Lovers' and he started with Part One.

A long time ago, the young Yang Hyun Suk had written this piece of music for his one and only love. But now, her new love was playing it just for her. What was this all about? Was this the power of jazz? The power of music? The power of love? The power of truth? Which one was it?

Sung Jae began with a prelude, and half way through, he played with a burst of energy. Then, he paused, and the lights gradually illuminated the whole stage. There behind him was the entire string orchestra. They began to play along with him. Yeon Mee was utterly astonished. Not only was Sung Jae playing for her but also the whole string orchestra! She was filled with emotions which were hard to contain. Her lips trembled as she tried to control them.

Sung Jae finished playing each version of Jazz Lovers, One, Two and Three...

The final melody resounded through the theatre. A long silence fell. And then, as Sung Jae stood up to bow, Yeon Mee smiled tearfully. They looked across at each other, and their eyes were shining...

26

Yeon Mee approached the gate where the name 'Yang Hyun Suk' was written. The name plate was ragged. The gate lost its balance and tilted to the left. The doorbell, too, was tattered with its wires sticking out. She hesitated outside, pacing up and down for a while before plucking up the courage to ring the bell.

"Who is it?" came a woman's voice from inside.

"Hello."

The gate opened. A woman stood at the entrance. It was Hyun Suk's daughter-in-law. She recognized Yeon Mee and was curious as to why she had come.

Jeong Soo's wife said, "Hello, how are you?"

"I'm doing all right. Thank you for asking."

"Come in, please." She called her husband, "We have a guest, dear!"

Jeong Soo appeared at the sliding door. He saw that it was Yeon Mee. He got up quickly, pulling his hair back behind his ears, and went across the deck to put on his shoes. He walked to the gate. He gave a respectful bow.

Yeon Mee said, "I'm sorry that I came here without notice."

"That's no problem. Why don't you come in?"

Yeon Mee came into the courtyard. She looked at the house and saw the workshop with some Haegeum tools. More were scattered over the yard.

"I just wanted to come and see your father's house." She said.

"Ah, yes."

Jeong Soo and his wife exchanged glances.

"Do come inside," he said, "The weather is very cold."

Jeong Soo's wife quickly ran inside the house to tidy up the rooms. Jeong Soo and Yeon Mee took their shoes off and stepped up on to the deck. Yeon Mee caught sight of a piano in the middle room and stopped to gaze at it. Then, she looked at the room on her left. Jeong Soo spoke to her, "That room was my father's room." Yeon Me walked towards it and asked, "Could I go inside?"

Jeong Soo said, "Sure. But the under-floor heating is turned off in there so it's very cold."

"That's all right. I'd like to see his room."

Yeon Mee walked inside and gazed around the room, looking at everything, then went to the middle room where the piano was.

"Was that your father's piano?" she asked.

"No, that's my daughter's piano."

"Does your daughter also play the Haegeum, as your father did?"

"No, she has only ever played the piano."

Yeon Mee was surprised. Jeong Soo said,

"My father broke that tradition. He asked me to consider having my daughter give up the Haegeum and play the piano instead."

Yeon Mee wanted to ask why but refrained. She walked over to the piano. Above it hung a family photo. There was silence in the room. Then Jeong Soo said, "Ever since meeting you at the hospital, I have been wanting to ask you something, but I haven't had a chance."

They looked at each other.

He said, "You told me at the hospital that you were helping my father because he and your father knew each other well. You mentioned that he was kind to your father. Could I please ask you what act of kindness he showed towards your father?"

Yeon Mee avoided Jeong Soo's eyes. Jeong Soo sensed that she was reluctant to answer him. He also looked away.

After a while, Yeon Mee said, "I want to answer that question you asked me before. I think I'm ready now, but it's a long answer. Would that be alright?"

"Um… If you feel uncomfortable you really don't have to." Firstly, she wanted to know what he knew about his mother. Hyun Suk already told her that he wouldn't know anything, but she still wanted to ask. She asked, "Where is your mother?"

Jeong Soo looked straight at her, finding it hard to answer her question. After a long pause, he asked a question, rather than a response, "Do you know my mother?" Yeon Mee was caught off guard and couldn't reply immediately. "Uh… yes. I do know your mother. It was long time ago though. How is she doing?"

"Sorry, I really don't know anything about my mother."

Yeon Mee just faced Jeong Soo in silence.

"I just know that she passed away soon after I was born."

"Who told you that?"

He felt that something was off and wondered why she had asked that. He didn't answer, avoiding her eyes.

"Is that what you believe?" she asked.

172

He quickly turned his head towards her.

They looked at each other and he saw that her eyes were red and that she was trembling. Jeong Soo felt as if someone had struck him on the back of the head. He saw that his wife, who had been glancing into the room, also had a shocked expression on her face. He looked out the window, bewildered. Out there, he saw a man standing waiting by a car. He realised that the man must be waiting for Yeon Mee. He turned to her and said, "A minute ago, I asked you why you were helping my father at the hospital. You don't need to give me any more details. But I would like to thank you for your kindness in exchange for the kindness of my father to your father."

They were silent again for a while. Yeon Mee looked at him, but Jeong Soo couldn't look at her.

He said, "I would like to play you one song before you leave, if you are okay with that? My father sometimes played it for our family."

Yeon Mee nodded.

He left and went to get his daughter from her room.

He reappeared with a Haegeum in one hand and his daughter's hand in the other. They went over to the piano. He lifted his daughter on to the piano stool and brought over another chair for himself. He tuned the Haegeum while his daughter waited. Yeon Mee thought about how pretty the little girl was. She smiled gently at her, then went over to be near her. In return, the girl smiled sweetly at her. Jeong Soo finished tuning and nodded to his daughter to start playing.

The song was *I Will Wait for You.*

Yeon Mee recognized that it was the same version Hyun Suk had played with her long ago when they had visited the secret piano place for the first time together. She could see that

Jeong Soo's daughter was a brilliant pianist—well beyond her years. She played perfectly. During the intermezzo, the little girl started to play openly and freely. She looked so professional! Yeon Mee was impressed. The child was playing a combination of bossa nova, tango, swing and standard jazz rhythms. Her arrangement of the song was exactly like Hyun Suk's. Yeon Mee felt tears stinging her eyes but she had promised herself not to cry in Jeong Soo's home. In spite of all her efforts, all of sudden, her eyes welled up with tears as she felt the beauty and sadness of the moment.

Outside, the snow was now falling much heavily than when she had arrived. And there was the Haegeum, the piano, jazz, her son, granddaughter, daughter-in-law, and Sung Jae…

The little girl had finished playing. Yeon Mee went over to her and picked her up, giving her a big hug and swinging her from side to side.

She put her down gently. Yeon Mee spoke in the silence.

"I have to go now."

Jeong Soo's wife quickly went out to the deck to shake the snow from Yeon Mee's shoes. Yeon Mee gave her a 'thank you' smile. The family prepared to accompany her to the gate. Suddenly, Jeong Soo asked her to wait, he had something to give her.

He came back, holding a piece of paper in his hand, which he gave to Yeon Mee.

"On the day, my father passed away, the police gave me this. I feel like I need to give this to you. It was the note he was holding when he took his own life."

Yeon Mee took the note. She opened it and read it. It was in her father's writing:

"*With true love, everything seems possible, but there is*

one pitfall. True love cannot control its own destiny. It was not your destiny to be with my daughter. But even now, I can see that your love for her has always been true through all the storms of life. That love is even more enduring than the love which gets what it wants. Yours is not a love that fades but one that stands the test of time. Hyun Suk, I am really sorry. Please try not to be too sad."

Yeon Mee's eyes filled with tears.

She looked up at the sky.

Snow was falling endlessly…